Black Friday at the Secondhand Bookworm

EMILY JANE BEVANS

DEDICATION

Dedicated to the memory of Kim Francombe

CONTENTS

ACKNOWLEDGMENTS

Thank you so much to my sister, Bernadette, who encourages me to write and who worked with me many times in the bookshop

1 THE BARGAIN BOOK YARD

"I don't think Castletown is the place for Black Friday." Nora Jolly said as she cut out an A4 'BLACK FRIDAY SALE' sign with a pair of blunt scissors.

"I agree. The town is full of antique shops and people ask for discounts in here every day anyway." Cara Jolly replied. "It just means they'll think we'll be obliged to oblige them."

"Imagine that." Nora sighed drearily.

The two young women were seated behind a cluttered counter in the front room of The Secondhand Bookworm, a three story shop filled with floors and stairwells bursting at the seams with books upon books, upon books. And more books.

Nora sat on a grey swivel chair with a stain on the back rest fabric that Georgina, the owner of The Secondhand Bookworm, suspected might be whisky, although Nora assured her no one ever drank whisky in the shop as far as she knew (it was actually coffee from when Cara nudged Nora's elbow)! Cara was perched on a rickety old wooden stool that wobbled a lot, (Georgina suspected the stool wobbled a lot because the staff played wobbling games) in front of a computer monitor that was currently displaying Skype chat.

It was Monday morning of the almost last week in November. There were four days until Black Friday and, because Georgina was dating an American named Troy, she was enthusiastic about having a Black Friday book sale in both her branches of bookshops.

Nora ran The Secondhand Bookworm in Castletown which was situated in the south coast county of Cole, and Cara, her sister-in-law, ran The Secondhand Bookworm in Seatown. The two shops were owned by Georgina Pickering who was the sister of Nora's kind-of-boyfriend, Humphrey. The Secondhand Bookworm unintentionally encouraged nepotism.

"Did you hear about the new part-timer?" Cara asked, tapping away on the Skype chat.

"Oh. Yes. Paperback Pam."

Cara laughed.

"Is that what she's called?"

"Only because she spent all her time in the paperback room when she worked with Georgina on Sunday."

"Well, her husband was a friend of Georgina's dad." Cara explained.

"Really?"

"So I expect Georgina is afraid to give her orders." Nora chuckled.

"Oh dear. Yes, she also worked with my mum for fifteen years in a primary school. I'm working with her here on Wednesday."

"That'll be nice."

The door opened. Usually there was an annoying two-toned door chime that accompanied it, but it had broken at the weekend. Nora was enjoying its absence.

"Morning." A man wrapped in an enormous knitted scarf greeted.

"Hello." Nora and Cara welcome in unison.

"It looks like it's going to rain. And it's supposed to be in for the week. So you may want to bring all your postcards and cheap offerings in from outside." He advised.

"Oh, thanks." Nora appreciated.

"Now, who wrote all of these books?" The man asked, looking around.

"Erm…lots of different authors." Nora replied.

"Not just one?"

Nora and Cara stared.

"No. They're all diverse authors and a variety of subjects. Our art section is there, Cole and topography is there by the door, those are our Folio Society books, under the counter at the front on those shelves are a mixture of leather runs, antiquarian and new Ordnance Survey maps, plus the shop goes back and up to the attic." Nora explained.

"My, my. How amusing. And where is your Bargain Book Yard?"

"Oh. I'm afraid it doesn't open until tomorrow." Nora replied.

"Oh, that is a shame."

"But we have lots of lovely books throughout The Secondhand Bookworm and they are all reasonably priced." Cara chipped in.

"Oh, I only like bargains. Thank you." The man said, turned around and left.

Nora and Cara looked at one another.

"Not a good start to the day." Nora said.

"Typical Monday." Cara sighed and bit into a cupcake.

"I hope The Bargain Book Yard is a good idea." Nora mused, finishing her sign. There was already a poster advertising Black Friday on the door, but Georgina had suggested making a sign that they could change daily in the countdown to Black Friday. Nora had printed out and laminated four numbers to place on the new poster each day, in front of where she had typed 'DAYS TO GO UNTIL BLACK FRIDAY!' It was in her favourite font, which was Garamond.

"I think it will be great." Cara said through her mouthful. "And it looks amazing."

"It does." Nora smiled wistfully.

The Bargain Book Yard was situated at the back of The Secondhand Bookworm through the small kitchen into a courtyard with a disused outside loo. The yard had been the site of several sewage disasters due to the Indian restaurant at the back pouring oil down their drains and causing massive clog-ups. It was also a place where slime and moss was profuse.

Since Halloween, Humphrey (Nora's kind-of-boyfriend) had spent several weeks scrubbing, disinfecting, cleaning and sprucing up the yard and then fixing tall heavy-duty wooden bookcases against all the walls. The walls that surrounded the yard were ancient and incorporated part of the Indian restaurant and flats, the estate agents next door and some of the antique shop on the other side of The Secondhand Bookworm.

There was a heavy bolted door that led down an alley to the Biffa rubbish bins (the bins could also be reached by walking around the block), so Humphrey had put a locked padlock on it to prevent people legging it with armfuls of bargain books. He had also fixed plastic covering over the whole area to protect it from the rain and pigeon droppings.

Nora had visited the Bargain Book Yard regularly as they had been filling up all the shelves with books. Georgina had had Nora and Cara go through both Bookworms and pull out anything that looked like it had sat there for a long time. She had also bought, for a song, several van loads of books from 'Universe of Books', a local book charity in Little Cove with whom she had a working relationship (and which Nora was convinced was a front for the Little Cove mafia). There was only one more van load to be delivered and Georgina and Humphrey were bringing it today. Then the Bargain Book Yard would be ready, with all books marked inside with red pencil instead of ordinary grey so that the staff would know which ones were from the yard and which ones from the rest of the shop.

The plan was to open up The Bargain Yard on Tuesday with 10% off all the books from there. Wednesday the discount would be 20%, Thursday 30% and then on Black Friday, 50% off. Georgina was convinced it would inspire a lot of trade and she had placed adverts in all the local papers.

There was already a three tiered wooden bargain trolley out on the street with the postcard spinners, black cheap paperback boxes and free maps. It too was serving as part of the Black Friday event.

"Humphrey made a good call covering the yard with that temporary plastic roofing." Cara admired, getting ready to bring in the postcards from outside as spots of rain began to fall.

Nora agreed.

"Yes, it's supposed to be a showery week. I expect it will sound like a tent out there."

"That'll be awesome!" Cara grinned.

Nora then squealed as something soft and furry brushed her leg.

"Arthur!" She gasped and laughed.

Cara giggled.

"I had forgotten all about you." Nora apologised, crouched down and began to fuss over a chubby bulldog in a red sweater with a white knitted bone on the front.

Arthur belonged to Cara, and Nora's brother Seymour, who was Cara's husband. Arthur was very sweet and liked to spend the day in the bookshops. He had a bed under the stairs in the Castletown branch where the staff kept their coats and bags, excess postcards, boxes of cheap paperbacks, boxes of free maps and bags of books people had left that they wished to sell for Georgina to look at. Arthur spent the day grunting, snuffling and snorting happily. He was also a loud snorer.

"Excuse me!" A woman with greasy grey pigtails screamed into the shop.

Cara paused in mid-bite. Nora straightened up.

"Can we help?" Nora asked politely.

"You can help yourselves. Your postcards and books out here are getting wet!" The woman said.

Arthur shuffled back to sit at Cara's feet, staring up at her cupcake, so Nora walked over to the door. Cara smirked to see Nora avoid part of the flagstone area by the Cole section. Since Halloween, Nora had learned of a covered well that housed the ghost of a trapped boy. It was said his crying could still be heard, so Nora didn't want to upset his spirit by stepping all over his haunted space.

"Thank you." Nora smiled at the pigtail lady.

She just stared and left.

It took Nora five minutes to wheel in the postcard spinners, throw in the sand puddings (little carrier bags filled with sand from rotted sandbags that were used as weights), push the new bargain trolley inside with a crash and unclip the four black boxes of cheap paperbacks which were fixed either side of the door. By the time she had finished the rain was falling in a steady stream.

"Shall I leave the free maps out?" Nora asked innocently.

"Best not." Cara grinned.

The free maps were annoying because the map of Castletown was tiny and folded inside the larger map of Seatown. People could never find it and often shouted '*you're out of free Castletown maps*' into the shop. Nora and her cousin Felix, who worked Saturdays at The Secondhand Bookworm, tried to invent ways to get rid of them as quickly as possible.

Grumbling, Nora ducked out into the rain, grabbed the little box and threw it behind the door.

Georgina had been going on bookshop van calls a lot with her boyfriend Troy to the houses of people wishing to sell large amounts of books. She had purchased four libraries of books from London, Fulking, Broadbridge Heath and Itchingfield. The books from Itchingfield had, ironically, come from a barn and were full of fleas. Nora bent down and scratched at her calves with a scowl.

"Honestly, I shall be pleased when all these books are on the shelves and fumigated. The flea powder Humphrey sprinkled everywhere doesn't seem to have killed them all."

The shop was higgledy-piggledy with books. They were piled on the floor, tottering in corners, stacked in walkways and stuffed onto every available shelf space. There were great mounds in front of the window display, all priced up but with nowhere to go. Nora felt smothered.

"At least Arthur's not infested." Cara said, tickling Arthur behind his ear.

He snuffled loudly, eyes closed. Nora giggled.

"Yes, that's true." She slapped her leg irritably.

A lady arrived.

"Hello, Gina."

Nora sighed inwardly.

Crossword-Lady was a regular who only popped in to ask answers to literary clue questions in her daily paper or occasionally buy books about donkeys. She insisted that Nora was working at The Secondhand Bookworm to research her latest film or TV role and was in fact the British actress called Gina McKee. Nothing Nora said could convince her otherwise.

"Good morning." Nora politely replied.

"Oh, so many books. It's like a library."

"Yes, that really is the only other definition." Nora smiled.

"Today's crossword question." Crossword-Lady said and unfolded her paper. "Moby Dick was original published in 1851 as The *blank*."

"The Whale?" Nora guessed.

"Is that a guess, Gina?" Crossword-Lady frowned.

"Erm…"

"I'll look it up!" Cara suggested, clicking onto Google.

"That's cheating." Crossword-Lady objected. "Honestly, Gina. It's a good thing you're researching your role here for so long if you still haven't learned everything there is to know about books."

"I don't think anyone could ever know…" Nora began but Crossword-Lady stared at her so she stopped talking.

"The Whale is correct." Cara announced.

Crossword-Lady sighed and wrote it into her puzzle.

"Well, that was a disappointment. I shall think twice about coming in tomorrow." She said, turned around and left.

Nora and Cara looked at one another.

"If I had known it would only take a guess at an answer to get rid of her I would have done that months ago." Nora smirked.

Cara laughed.

"I know! You'll have to make up some obviously wrong answers."

"I should do. She is driving me to despair." Nora mused.

"You could also hide next time she comes in and we can say you've researched your movie role enough and are now filming." Cara suggested.

Nora grinned.

She picked up her poster and finished cutting it out and then hunted around for the best place to display it in the window.

"There are some requests from Seatown." Cara then read. "A customer is looking for any novels by Michael Connelly. The Harry Bosch series."

"Shall I go and have a look?"

"No, it's okay. I'll go." Cara said and set off.

Nora tacked her poster in the window and was just cuddling Arthur when the telephone began to ring.

"Good morning, The Secondhand Bookworm." Nora greeted the caller.

"It's me!" Georgina shrieked.

"Oh, hello." Nora replied and sat down on the swivel chair.

"We're on our way but there's a big queue. A tractor has overturned."

"Oh dear."

"Hmm. There are bales of hay and a squashed scarecrow in the road." Georgina pointed out, ignoring Nora's laugh. "Oh. Really? Humphrey's taking photos for you."

"Thanks." Nora grinned.

"I just had Niall on the phone, from Salmon postcards."

"Oh, yes?"

"They're going out of business."

Nora blinked.

"What?"

"Yes. Isn't that insane. We sell hundreds of their postcards! They're not making anymore, *at all*, even though they supply shops all over the country. It's mad. So I've asked for their last remaining stock of Castletown and Seatown postcards and a new postcard spinner."

"A new spinner? Why?"

"Oh, I just wanted one!" Georgina defended. "He seemed keen to sell it to me cheap."

Nora smirked.

"Okay."

"So we'll up the price on the cards after a while."

"Wow. End of an Era."

"Don't pretend you aren't happy about it."

"Alright." Nora said and cheered.

"Hmm. There'll be no point selling stamps either. I guess it's down to the new technology. People send photos on the social networks now, and prices of stamps are a joke."

"We certainly haven't been selling as many as in past years." Nora said.

"Oh! We're moving. We'll be with you shortly."

"Okay."

Nora rang off and sat staring at the postcards spinners happily. She found them a nuisance, but she expected they would hang around for a few more years yet.

Cara returned.

"We have 'The Concrete Blond', 'Nine Dragons' and 'The Wrong Side of Goodbye' in paperback." Cara told Nora cheerfully.

"Oh good."

She sat down to reply to their colleague Roger who was working with their colleague Betty in Seatown.

"Back in a minute." Nora said and fled up the stairs.

When she came back down, Cara was eating an Easter egg. Nora did a double take.

"Where did you get that?"

Cara laughed.

"I found it in a box I hadn't gotten around to unpacking after I moved in with Seymour. It's still before its use by date."

Nora smirked.

"I thought I'd put this in the window." She said and held up a large, wide paperback she had fetched.

"Scarecrows. By Gregory Holyoake." Cara read and stared at the photograph of a very ugly, rather scary scarecrow on the front.

"Why?"

"Georgina is on her way and said there was a squashed scarecrow in the road."

Cara almost choked laughing.

A very skinny woman, like a skeleton, strolled into The Secondhand Bookworm. She had cropped bright blond hair.

"Oh! It's pink in here." She said in a gravelly voice.

Nora prickled. For a moment she had thought the woman had said 'it's warm in here!' which was a comment that plagued Nora over the winter, when customers arrived wrapped up like Eskimos and complained that the bookshop was warmer than outside. She even made a tally chart about it each year and in fact had printed it out already ready to stick on the wall under the alarm pad and start tallying.

"Oh, yes it is." Cara agreed brightly.

The front of The Secondhand Bookworm had been painted pink to match the pink replacement carpet a couple of years ago by Cara's uncle. Some people found it either amusing or shocking, while most didn't even notice.

"I love it!" Skeleton-Lady exclaimed. "Now, do you have any books about the art of Erwin Wurm?"

"Oh! Do you mean the pickle book?" Nora asked.

"The what?" Skeleton-Lady was bemused.

Nora walked over to the art section, crouched down and scanned the shelf where artist sculpture books were kept. A large white tome with a big green gherkin on the front was easily located. She pulled it out, stood up and showed the lady.

"Edwin Wurm. And his incredible pickles." Nora smirked.

Skeleton-Lady gasped.

"May I look?"

"Please do."

Nora passed her the book and grinned at Cara. When the book had first come in, Nora and her sister Heather, who worked for Georgina ad hoc in The Secondhand Bookworm, had spent a good hour giggling over the photographs of Edwin Wurm's sculptures, which included a man standing in a bucket with a bucket on his head, a man with his head buried in a wall, someone with every orifice of their face filled with stationery objects such as a stapler, pens and pencil sharpeners, someone trapped in a chair and a lady laying down on loads of oranges. It was hilarious.

They had put it in the window display until they had grown fed up with the constant exclamations of '*why is there a pickle on the front of that book?*' sailing into the shop from outside.

"Oh, I love this. I must have it." Skeleton-Lady decided. She brought it to the counter. "How much is it?"

"Thirty five pounds." Nora replied, opening the cover and pointing to the pencil price.

"That's a good deal. Do you take cards?"

"We do." Cara smiled.

"And is this part of your Black Friday bargain week?"

Nora's smile faded.

"Unfortunately not. Our bargain books are located in our yard at the back of the shop, but it won't be opened until tomorrow."

"Oh that's fine. I thought this would be too good for a discount."

The lady paid, showed them several examples of sculpture that made Cara choke and Nora laugh, and then she left happily.

"A good sale for the start of the day." Nora said, placing her scarecrow book in the window.

"Not bad for a Monday morning." Cara agreed.

The sound of snoring filled the air. Arthur had gone to sleep.

While they waited for Georgina and Humphrey to arrive with the last of the bargain book stock for the yard, seeing as there was no room on any of the shelves for the piles of books throughout the shop and nothing really to do, Nora pulled a book she was reading from her bag, stepping over Arthur to reach it.

"Ooooh. Which one are you on now?" Cara asked, interested.

"Book four. Deacon Victor turns to Crime." Nora said, holding up a vintage-looking tome.

"I can't wait to read them." Cara grinned.

The book was part of a six volume series of novels written by a Catholic priest decades ago and privately printed. Nora had been given six boxes, containing fifty copies of each novel, on a call over Halloween, along with the copyright which the late author's brother had posted to her. They were crime mystery stories like G.K. Chesterton's Father Brown novels, with a priest of a parish in a village close to Castletown solving mysteries and happenings in his church. Nora had organised a Book Club to start in the middle of December in which members would read together and discuss the novels.

She was reading them first herself to get acquainted with them.

"They're really good." She told Cara, settling down in the swivel chair. "I think you'll enjoy them."

"How many people have signed up for the Book Club now?"

"Six."

"Including the Duke of Cole?"

"Yes." Nora nodded, hiding her pleased smile.

The Duke of Cole lived in the newly built and renovated gothic castle located in a large estate that overlooked the town. He had moved in last year and had met Nora at Christmas after a very heavy snowfall. The Secondhand Bookworm had been the only shop open in the town and the Duke had come across her when he had escaped his castle alone to explore. They had struck up a friendship and Nora had since visited the Duke's private library and was collecting First Edition P. G Wodehouse novels for him. When he had that heard that Nora was hosting a Book Club he had been the second person to sign up. Felix had been the first because he had been working with Nora when she had made her poster.

"I'd like to have one more member so we will be a group of eight. But no more than ten." Nora decided.

"Sounds good." Cara smiled.

"I will make the copies of the first book we will be reading available at the end of the week. Book one is called 'The Missing Candlesticks'."

"I'm so looking forward to it!" Cara said enthusiastically.

Nora grinned.

Nora and Cara had only enjoyed five minutes of peace and quiet when The Secondhand Bookworm calls van pulled up on the double yellow lines outside the shop. It then reversed slowly into a sort of parking space half outside the antique shop next door.

Bangs and crashes, sawing and hammering had been coming from the shop next door for two weeks. The owner was currently renovating the entire building and he and his wife were being a general nuisance, moaning about not being able to have access to their walls that were in the bookshop yard and trying to use the bookshop window to sell enormous items such as what they insisted was an Enigma machine, as well as a huge printing press. Felix rudely called the woman 'Hatchet Face' because she refused to say hello to him.

"Ah, they're here." Cara noticed.

Nora slipped her book on the top shelf under the counter where books reserved for customers were kept in large clear bags.

"I suppose we should help them unload."

"Yeah." Cara yawned, stretching.

Humphrey walked past the window carrying three boxes at once.

"Show off!" Nora greeted him fondly.

Humphrey grinned.

"Morning." He replied, hoisting the boxes into the shop and depositing them on the carpet. "The last of these flipping bargain books. Ugh. I hope I never see another book again as long as I live."

Cara laughed.

"How will you visit Nora? She works in a bookshop!"

"I'll close my eyes." He said, leaned in and kissed Nora's cheek fondly.

In return she popped a stick of liquorice between his teeth. Humphrey cheered up considerably.

"Morning, Arthur!" Humphrey greeted as he chewed, leaning over the counter top.

Arthur snored.

"Good luck waking that lump up." Cara said fondly and stepped out onto the street where Georgina was rummaging loudly in the van.

"How's it been this morning?" Humphrey asked Nora, chewing on his liquorice stick and gazing at her affectionately.

"Slow. Quiet. But pleasant."

Humphrey grinned.

"Are you going to help me put these books on the shelves out there then?" He asked hopefully.

"Of course." Nora smiled.

"Great. How about I make a round of tea first?"

"Thanks. I'll go and grab a couple of boxes from the van."

"See you in a minute." Humphrey nodded and headed through a walkway that led deeper into The Secondhand Bookworm.

A customer entered the shop.

"Oh. Hello." Nora smiled politely.

"Cookery books!" The old lady demanded. She was followed by a very small man who was tailing her like an abused puppy.

"Our cookery section is on the next floor." Nora explained.

"Oh I don't do stairs!" The woman snapped. "Maurice. Come!"

The man obediently turned around and they both left.

Nora had only taken three more steps towards the door when another customer arrived.

"I've come to cheer myself up." He said. "Have you got any comedy books because my wife died last week?"

Nora stared.

"Oh, I'm terribly sorry to hear that. We have a humour section on the next floor."

"That should do it." He said, followed Nora's directions and was soon creaking up the stairs.

Nora finally made it to the doorstep only to be faced by Cara passing her two boxes of books.

"There are loads! Fortunately they're all already priced in red pencil." Cara explained.

"Yes. It took me hours! Morning, Nora." Georgina's voice sounded from behind another tower of books. "I'll place these by the door and you can move them all inside."

"Morning. Okay." Nora agreed, taking the boxes from Cara first, who turned and hurried back to the van.

It took a full ten minutes to unload. By the end of it there was a wall of blue boxes in front of the piles of books already stacked on the floor, so that there was only a small corridor leading to the back of the shop. Nora felt like hyperventilating because it was very claustrophobic.

Humphrey had made tea and finished his liquorice.

"How about a donut each before we get moving these?" He suggested, placing the mugs in a row on the counter top.

"Yes please!" Cara's voice sounded from behind part of the wall of boxes. "Wow. You have some good sets here. Great prices."

"Yes, I thought we'd better be a couple of classes above a charity shop in the Bargain Book Yard." Georgina said, making a fuss over Arthur who had shuffled into the corridor to explore the upheaval. "I've marked them so that even with the 50% off on Black Friday we will make a profit."

"Donut?" Humphrey asked Nora.

"Thanks." Nora smiled.

"Back in a minute." He said, kissing her cheek again.

He squeezed past Cara, who had emerged, and disappeared out of the shop.

"Shall we start carrying these out into the Bargain Book Yard?" Cara suggested.

"If you want." Georgina pulled a face.

"Don't tell me you've actually, finally, had enough of books?" Nora teased.

"Well, I have." Georgina admitted. "Wait until you've had some tea and donuts before moving the boxes into the yard. You'll need your strength."

"Okay." Nora agreed, peering into one of the top boxes.

They were a variety of books, nice condition, but very general.

Georgina had discovered 'Deacon Victor turns to Crime' and was flicking through it with interest.

"If you decide to get these reissued in modern paperback, Nora, I'd be keen on stocking them." She said.

"Really? I'll see how my Book Club goes and let you know."

Georgina smiled.

Nora, Cara and Georgina sipped their tea and chatted, waiting for Humphrey to return with donuts, while numerous customers appeared. The rain was falling steadily outside so Cara borrowed Nora's large cream umbrella to take Arthur along the road to relieve himself. When she returned, the donuts had arrived.

"I can bring them in, they're in my car." A woman in a horrible brown mac was saying to Georgina.

"Well, as you can see I'm quite swamped at the moment. It would be better if we made an appointment."

"Well, I can't keep them in my boot. I need to do my Tesco shopping." The woman moaned indignantly.

"How about you drive over to my Seatown branch? I can meet you there." Georgina suggested.

"Oh. Yes, I suppose I could do that. Now?"

"I can be there in about half an hour."

"Ten minutes, the way Georgina drives." Humphrey muttered to Nora.

Nora smirked.

"Alright. Thank you. I'll head over."

"Just pull up before the shop and I'll tell my colleague Roger to come out and make a start looking through."

"Will do." The woman said, turned around and left.

Georgina gulped down her tea.

"I'll leave you here Humphrey."

"No problem. I expect I'll be here for the day helping with the yard."

"Great. Thanks." Georgina appreciated.

Humphrey smiled at Nora who grinned. Cara smirked, looking between them.

Georgina skyped Roger and Betty to tell them about the lady with the books for sale. She then gathered her things.

"Have a good day. I'll try to pop in this afternoon or at some point to see the yard. Love the signs, Nora. Well done."

"Thanks." Nora nodded, biting into a donut.

Georgina left hastily just as another customer stepped into the shop. He had mad white curls and a tiny moustache.

"Wow. Are you moving in?" He asked, staring at the boxes.

"Oh. No, we're just sorting out stock." Nora replied. "Can we help?"

"The Iliad and the Odyssey by Homer?"

Cara jumped up to show him where any copies would be.

"How do?"

A regular customer had arrived. She was a small lady with cropped grey hair and large glasses. She collected bird books.

"Hello, Mrs Alton." Nora smiled.

The man whose wife had died and who had asked for any funny books to cheer himself up came into the front room, carrying a pile of 'Mad Magazines'.

"I found these." He told Nora, smirking.

"Oh, yes. Mad."

He had four issues of the American magazine with the boy mascot Alfred E. Neuman on the cover in various situations. Nora took them and ran the prices through the till while Mrs Altman examined a new copy of 'The Woman in Black' on the counter top. Next she picked up a book about Australian flowers.

"I went on a six week tour of Australia a few years ago." Mrs Altman said as the Mad man left.

"Wow."

"When I flew to Perth I had a pain in my leg. In the end, my tour guide took me to a doctor. The doctor said: '*Don't move! You have a blood clot.*' So I had to have injections for the rest of the trip."

"Oh my goodness!" Nora winced.

"Up I go." She said and began towards the walkway leading to the stairs.

Humphrey and Nora looked at one another.

Cara returned with the Homer customer who stood and read them paragraphs from the Iliad until he left.

"Shall we start taking these through then?" Nora suggested.

"Let's get cracking." Humphrey agreed, flexing his biceps.

Cara sat down in the swivel chair.

"I'll leave you two love birds to it." She grinned.

"Thanks." Nora smirked, picking up two boxes.

Cara placed the shop keys on top of the top box so Nora could unlock the outer kitchen door and open up the Bargain Book Yard. Humphrey hoisted up three boxes and followed her through the walkway.

The kitchen was a small annex which literally only had enough room to stand and make a cup of tea in. There was a sink, short fridge, bin and two wall cupboards full of mugs. A tiny stool was kept in there if people wanted to eat in the kitchen. Also an oil heater. The roof was made of Pyrex so it was perpetually cold.

Everything had been tidied away and mats put down on the laminated floor in anticipation of a flow of customer traffic leading up to Black Friday. Nora unlocked the kitchen door and entered the Bargain Book Yard.

The Bargain Book Yard had the atmosphere of a large and exciting marquee. The tall, heavy duty bookcases that Humphrey had fixed all around the walls were almost full of books. They had been sorted into subject sections. There were also three small tables dotted about, piled high with interesting tomes, maps and comics. The floor had been swept and scrubbed clean, although a few weeds had rebelliously grown up among the cobbles and flagstones. The temporary roofing was firm and secure and the rain pattered down upon it pleasantly and weaved in special channels to the uncovered drains. It was light and airy. The outside brick loo had been decorated with posters. The door was locked but a sign on it read: '*Please do not use the loo*!'

"You've done such a good job out here." Nora praised Humphrey, putting her boxes down in the middle of the room.

"Thanks." He appreciated, stacking his boxes next to hers.

"Do you think Georgina will let us keep it like this?"

There was a bubbling sound of water coming from the corner of the yard. The drains from the Indian restaurant, flats, estate agents and The Secondhand Bookworm all flowed into and out of the bookshop yard.

Nora grimaced slightly, remembering several poops that had floated by when there had been blocked sewers.

"I'm not sure." Humphrey shrugged and then wrapped his arms around Nora, spinning her around and down so that he leaned over her.

"Humphrey!" Nora rebuked on a laugh.

"This is nice. Getting to spend the day with you."

"As long as you don't distract me from working." Nora said, kissed his nose and wiggled free.

The estate agents had fitted a large and unsightly air conditioning unit on their wall and during the summer it belted out loud, warm air. They paid five hundred pounds a year rent for the wall space to The Secondhand Bookworm and had kindly agreed not to use it during Black Friday week. It was lovely and peaceful.

"Let's bring all the boxes through from the front so the customers can move." Nora suggested.

She and Humphrey headed back to where Cara was serving an extremely large man who looked wedged between the counter and the wall of bargain books.

"Erm…" Cara was looking baffled. "What was the question again?"

"Who wrote 'Jane Austen'?" The man asked.

Humphrey's laugh became a cover-up cough as he lifted three more boxes.

"Well, Jane Austen wrote Jane Austen." Cara replied, giving Nora a look.

"Really?" He seemed fascinated.

"Yes. She wrote about seven novels."

"Huh, you don't say."

Nora and Humphrey quickly carried their boxes away, smirking about leaving Cara manning the desk.

It took them a while to cart everything into the yard. When they returned with the last haul, a man was pulling books out of one of the boxes in the middle.

"Oh. Excuse me. Sorry, the yard isn't open until tomorrow." Nora explained.

"I would like to buy this." The man held up a large paperback copy of The Lord of the Rings trilogy.

"Oh. Well, you can but we can't give a discount on it until tomorrow."

"That's okay. I'll pay the price that's written on it." The man said.

Nora escorted him back to Cara and explained so Cara ran the price through the till and the man went off happily. Cara rolled her eyes.

"Honestly, they need watching all the time." She said, patting Arthur.

"Hmm. Mind if we get unpacking?"

"No go ahead. I'm fine here." Cara nodded and went back to playing Solitaire on the computer.

Nora headed back to the Bargain Book Yard.

The boxes had been sorted into topics so it was easy to start unpacking the books. They had arranged the yard in alphabetical order of subjects, so architecture began to the left of the bolted and padlocked door. Next was art. The books were general and nothing particularly special, but they were all in nice condition and priced well. Nora began to unpack and shelve a box of cookery books while Humphrey started on a box of equestrian.

"Do you remember our snowman?" Humphrey asked, perusing a large book about Shire horses.

"How could I forget?" Nora chuckled.

"I hope it snows again over Christmas. We can make him a sibling." Humphrey mused.

The smell of cigarette smoke wafted over them. Nora glowered towards the bookcases covering the frosted windows of the Indian restaurant. The windows still opened a fraction against the backs of the cases and the workers who took their cigarette breaks still insisted on blowing smoke through the crack. Nora waved her hand in front of her face and coughed.

"I hope that doesn't put our customers off." She lamented.

"We can get some air fresheners?" Humphrey suggested.

"I think that would be a good idea. Grrr." Nora agreed.

He grinned, adding a run of cheap Wisden Cricketer Almanacs to the sports section from his next box. In the end, he unlocked the door to the bins and let some fresh air into the yard.

A customer stepped in from the kitchen.

"Sorry, but we're not opening this yard until tomorrow." Nora called.

"It looks great. Do you have any Lilliput Lane houses for sale?"

Nora dropped the books she was holding.

"Pardon?"

"Lilliput Lane houses." The man repeated.

"Books about them?"

"No, the houses."

"Sorry, no we don't." Nora assured.

"Can I look at that book there?"

"I'm afraid not. This section is closed at the moment." Nora insisted.

"Just that book…there…" He walked over to the nearest case and pulled one off.

Humphrey's shoulders shook with laughter.

"Mind if I buy this?"

"It won't be discounted."

"Fair enough." He said, turned around and left.

"We need to lock the kitchen door! Next they'll be making themselves cups of tea." Nora exclaimed.

Humphrey agreed.

By lunchtime, Nora and Humphrey had unpacked and shelved all the books. They decided to display books on the tables and put up black and white 'Black Friday' bunting after lunch, so returned to the front of the shop where Cara was speaking with a group of customers buying postcards.

"Does the Duke live at the castle?" A man with a strong German accent asked.

"Does he ever." Humphrey muttered in Nora's ear as he leaned over to hang up the shop keys.

Nora glanced at him and smiled. It was no secret between them that Nora had a crush on the handsome Duke of Cole. What annoyed Humphrey though was that he suspected the Duke had a crush on Nora.

"Yes. He lives in part of the castle that remains unopened to the public." Cara explained.

"Why is the castle closed now?"

"It's closed from October to April every year." Cara said.

"Why?" A woman demanded.

"I think the castle gets a good cleaning, you know, like polishing chandeliers and cleaning furniture, and any renovations I expect." Cara said. "We have some castle guides if you're interested."

The group 'oooed' so Nora fetched them off of the shelf in the Cole section and handed them around.

"I heard the Duke has a hunchback." One lady said.

Humphrey snorted into his tea.

"No." Nora assured.

Cara giggled.

"Oh. Isn't he about a hundred years old?"

"He's thirty two." Nora said, and smiled apologetically at Humphrey.

Humphrey rolled his eyes.

"What is Black Friday?" The last woman asked.

"Black Friday is the day after the American Day of Thanksgiving." Cara explained. "It marks the first day of Christmas shopping so many retailers start their discounts and have promotional sales."

"You live and learn." The man said, waved his small brown bag of postcards and stamps and headed off.

Humphrey fussed over Arthur while Nora and Cara added up the sales so far.

"At least the front of the shop is now clear of boxes." Nora said, relieved.

"Yep. And there is a lot of interest in Black Friday." Cara nodded.

"Good. Would you like to go for lunch first?"

"I've been eating all these crisps, so you guys can go first if you like."

"Thanks, Cara. I'll take Nora to The Knight's Table across the road." Humphrey decided, standing up.

"Oooh. Thanks." Nora smiled.

The Knight's Table was a new restaurant that had arrived. It was on the other side of the road from Nora's flat, several doors down from The Duke's Pie restaurant, and now in competition with all the eateries of Castletown.

Humphrey passed Nora her scarf and bag and then helped her shrug into her coat.

"Have a nice lunch." Cara grinned.

"See you in a bit." Nora nodded, picked up her umbrella and Humphrey took hold of Nora's free hand, leading her from The Secondhand Bookworm so as to fill up with fuel and then continue working in the Bargain Book Yard that afternoon.

2 BOOKWORMS ON ICE

Castletown had a very autumnal feel about it. A fresh tumble of autumn leaves had been swept into piles by Hugh the street cleaner, who was currently using a machine to blow more fallen leaves along the gutter while glaring at cars passing by. Shop window displays contained garlands of red, yellow and orange leaves and fruit as well as autumn themed wares.

Foods and drinks such as pumpkin soups, mulled wine, hot chocolate and autumn lunches were being served, and autumn events were taking place in the town hall, like the honey festival, cider fayre and a woodturning workshop. Signs were up about the town advertising the 'Autumn Square Dancing and Folk Festival and Food Fayre' taking place in the town square on Saturday. There were also lots of posters up for the Giant Pumpkin Competition that would be part of the 'Autumn Supper and Festival' taking place in the castle on Wednesday evening.

Georgina had bought tickets for all the bookshop staff to attend the castle festival (Humphrey included) and had cancelled their accounting lessons with her accountant that week. The Secondhand Bookworm accountant was teaching Georgina, Nora, Cara, Betty and Roger how to use 'Sage', an accounting programme that was useful and more advanced for use in The Secondhand Bookworm shops.

Devon, the accountant, had such enormous teeth that he distracted them as he attempted to show them all how to use the complicated software during a three hour long lesson on Wednesday evenings. They had had two out of six lessons so were pleased to be missing one that week. Georgina had also invited everyone to a Thanksgiving dinner on Thursday night at her house, hosted by Troy, her American boyfriend.

The first of the Christmas decorations were beginning to appear about Castletown so that everything looked twinkly and exciting.

Marbles was a shop located opposite The Secondhand Bookworm run by a scruffy man named Stan. Stan positioned a gold mannequin next to the entrance of his shop every day and liked to display various clothing on The Woman in Gold. Today she wore a large black hat with autumn fruits around the brim, a long fake fur coat and Steampunk goggles. Humphrey and Nora took it in turns to pose beside her and take photos.

"We should go on the Deer Rut Safari in the park tomorrow evening." Humphrey suggested as they stood beneath Nora's umbrella to read a poster on the window of The Knight's Table next to the menu.

"Really?"

"It looks great." Humphrey had to admit.

"I heard that the Duke's re-wilding initiative of the parklands on his estate is going well." Nora mused.

"He's bought two pinzgauers and had them kitted out for his gamekeepers to take people on safaris." Humphrey relayed, reluctantly impressed. "Apparently the red fallow deer on his land put on the most amazing antler battles during the rut season."

"I'd like to see that." Nora smiled.

"I'll get us some tickets. It's the first time it's happening so there might not be any left. But I know Spike, one of the gamekeepers, so it shouldn't be a problem for us to go along. I think he keeps a few back to sell on the side."

"Great." Nora nodded, entering the restaurant. "Did you hear that an ice-rink is being set up by the river today? It'll stay until the New Year."

"We have to go on that!" Humphrey exclaimed loudly, and then cleared his throat as a medieval buxom wench approached them to show them to a table.

"Did you know that deer antlers grow half an inch a day?" Nora whispered to Humphrey.

"I'll have the venison." He teased.

Nora slapped his arm.

Over lunch, Humphrey showed Nora all the photos he had taken on the way to The Secondhand Bookworm that morning of the overturned tractor, scattered bales of hay and especially the squashed scarecrow in the road. Nora almost choked on her steak pie and chips with laughter.

After they had left The Knight's Table they took a quick detour to the river so as to check out the ice rink. It had been erected inside a large white marquee and a man was skating about on it accompanied by disco music and strobe lighting. It cost five pounds per person which included the hire of ice-skates. When they returned to The Secondhand Bookworm, Nora told Cara about the ice rink. She squealed with excitement, which woke Arthur up, telephoned Seymour and arranged a family group outing for after work.

Nora stood scratching her calves while Cara got ready to take Arthur for a walk and grab some lunch. A woman walked past the window wearing a cardboard hat with the words '*Jesus Loves You*' written on it. She had a table of teacups in the antique centre and liked to evangelise. Humphrey stared at her as he stood eating another donut.

"Where's your Bargain Book Yard?" A man in a camouflage jacket asked.

"It's in the back but it isn't open until tomorrow." Nora replied.

"That's a shame." The man said.

He decided to browse the Folio Society books instead.

"How much for cash?" A second man asked.

He dumped a pile of books onto the cash book on the counter, trying to intimidate Nora with his bushy browed eyes.

"I'm sorry but I can't change the prices of the books." Nora explained.

"Hogwash." The man scowled.

"It isn't my shop." Nora added warily.

"These are marked too high. I won't pay a penny less than thirty pounds." He threatened.

"Let me check them for you."

"I demand to speak to the owner."

"Hello. I'm the owner." Humphrey lied politely.

Cara left with Arthur, smirking.

"Oh." The man's bushy eyebrows danced up and down.

"Let me have a look. Excuse me, my child." Humphrey said to Nora and wiped the sugar and donut jam from his fingers on a wet wipe, purposefully taking his time. He began to hum, cleaning under his finger nails. Bushy-Eyebrows sighed impatiently.

"Now. Hmm. Yes, yes. I see." Humphrey muttered, leaning over the small pile of books. "Tum te tum. Te tum. Te tum te tum."

"Well?" Bushy-Eyebrows demanded.

"I can do these for thirty three pounds, sir." Humphrey finally offered.

"Humph. Well…"

"That's my only offer." Humphrey assured.

"Fine!" The man snapped and dug out his wallet.

Nora watched Humphrey run the sales through the till, bag up the books and bid the man a nice day. When he had gone, Humphrey turned to Nora.

"The books actually came to thirty three pounds anyway." He said.

Nora laughed, writing the sale down in the cash book.

"Does Georgina mind you impersonating her?"

"Yes." Humphrey nodded.

Nora grinned.

"HELLO!"

Humphrey and Nora flinched as an old man stepped down into the shop. Nora recognised him as Shouting Stanley, a customer who appeared occasionally and shouted everything he said because he was deaf. He was also missing several fingers. Humphrey's mouth dropped open.

"Hello." Nora replied.

"I'VE COME TO FIND SOME BOOKS BY THOMAS HARDY. YOU KNOW, BOOKS LIKE 'UNDER THE GREENWOOD TREE' AND OTHER CLASSICS. I'M DEAF SO PLEASE SPEAK UP. PARDON?"

Nora cleared her throat.

"HARDY WAS HIGHLY CRITICAL OF VICTORIAN SOCIETY AND MANY YOUNGER POETS LOOKED ON HIM AS A MENTOR. I'M INTERESTED IN HIS 'FAR FROM THE MADDING

CROWD' AND HIS 'TESS OF THE
D'UBURVILLES'. HAVE YOU EVER READ THEM
YOUNG LADY?" Shouting Stanley shouted.

Humphrey winced.

"Yes." Nora replied.

"PARDON?"

"Yes."

"PARDON?"

Nora nodded.

He cupped one of his gloved, fingerless hands over
one ear.

"I'M DEAF!"

"We have some paperbacks."

"PARDON?"

Nora picked up a pen and wrote it on a piece of
paper. Shouting Stanley leaned in and read it and then
laughed.

"IT'S A GOOD JOB I CAN READ."

Nora smiled.

Shouting Stanley's fingerless gloves had been sewn
up over the useless finger-holes and threads were
sticking out at funny angles.

"CAN YOU SHOW ME THE WAY? PARDON?
I'M DEAF!"

"I'LL TAKE YOU SIR!" Humphrey yelled back,
making Shouting Stanley jump.

"WOULD YOU, LAD? THANK YOU! I SEE YOU
HAVE A COPY OF THE TELL-TALE HEART BY
EDGAR ALLEN POE ON YOUR DESK." He noticed.
He roared with laughter. "A MODERN DAY FABLE
THAT CAPTURES GUILT AND CONFESSION. IF
ONLY PEOPLE ABIDED BY IT TODAY THERE
WOULDN'T BE SO MUCH SELF HARM."

Nora smiled politely and Humphrey led the way.
When she heard them creaking and climbing and
shouting all the way to the attic room, Nora laughed to

herself. She could still hear them in the background as another customer arrived. When she saw who it was, Nora inwardly groaned.

The young man was a local who only seemed to visit the shop when he was drunk or high on magic mushrooms. He also smelt strongly of Nag Champa. Ironically he often visited The Secondhand Bookworm at around the same time as Shouting Stanley and brought just as much chaos. He liked to spend lots of money on art books and sometimes psychology, but only when he was delirious. He seemed delirious.

"Hello." Drunk-Boy said, shuffling really quickly into the shop and heading to the art section. "Hello. Haha. Hello."

"Hello." Nora replied warily.

Drunk-Boy wore a long green parka, jeans, boots and his hair was wild. He gave Nora a shifty look and opened a can of coke that he whipped from his pocket.

"No drinking in here." She told him.

"Sssss. Mickey Mouse state." He objected, took a sip and grinned.

Nora saw that his eyes were bloodshot and bleary. She sighed.

"Anything on Andy Shaw?" He asked. "Yeah. He's a British artist, right…a book with photos of his paintings? Like 'Modern Home with Shark Pool' or 'French Bulldog cruising down the boulevard'? I've got money."

Nora watched him pull a wad of notes from the waistband of his jeans.

"Are you sure?" Nora asked, hating taking money from him when he was high.

"Wha'?" Drunk-Boy's mouth dropped open. "Why don't you want my money? Show me the money!" He burst out laughing.

"Well, I don't think I've seen anything about Andy Shaw." Nora admitted.

Drunk-Boy slurped his coke and then belched.

"That is rude!" Nora exclaimed.

"Sorry. Yeah, sorry." He said, staring at her with glittering eyes and then he covered his mouth with his notes.

Nora tried not to laugh.

"I'll look for myself then." Drunk-Boy said and turned back to the art section, sipping his coke noisily.

Nora shook her head.

"You're boring." He muttered.

"I saw you in church last week." Nora then said.

Drunk-Boy spun around and stared.

"What?" He asked, amazed and amused.

"You came in and sat down at the side. And you were making comments. And then you left at the Gospel." Nora informed him.

He burst out laughing.

"Man, was I high? You Catholics are high. I mean, wow, your church. *Transubstantiation*. Yeah. It blows the mind." He admired.

Nora smiled.

"Yes, it does rather." She said.

He covered his mouth, guiltily.

"I didn't do anything bad did I?" He asked.

"No." Nora assured. "You were just…loud."

"That's mad." Drunk-Boy finished his coke and went back to looking at the art books.

Nora heard Humphrey and Shouting Stanley heading slowly down and pausing to look at the Wordsworth books. A moment later, Drunk-Boy grabbed a handful of art books.

"These, please." He dropped three large books on the counter.

Nora drew them towards her. The first was a hardback copy of 'Gendun Chopel - Tibet's First Modern Artist' priced at thirty pounds. The second was a book about the art of Tracy Emin and the third a book about Damien Hirst. The total came to seventy five pounds. Drunk-Boy waved the money fiercely at her. Nora sighed and rang the prices through the till.

"Do you need a bag?"

"You and your plastic." He frowned.

"Okay." Nora shrugged, not even bothering to point out the cotton and jute bags that were for sale.

"The physical impossibilities of death in the mind of someone living." Drunk-Boy said, pointing to the Damien Hirst book.

Nora sighed.

He gathered his books, left his coke and staggered off, belching.

Nora shook her head, popped the coke can in the bin and wrote down the sales just as Humphrey and Shouting Stanley returned, loaded with books.

"YOUR FRIEND WANTS TO SELL ME THESE. I WON'T RESIST BECAUSE I LIKE A GOOD YARN!" Shouting Stanley yelled.

"Oh. Great." Nora nodded.

"PARDON?"

Nora just smiled.

Shouting Stanley bought his books, Humphrey bagged them up and as he left shouting, Cara and Arthur returned. Once Cara had settled down, Nora and Humphrey headed back to the Bargain Book Yard and spent the rest of the afternoon preparing it for the grand opening the following day.

The black and white 'Black Friday' bunting looked effective in the Bargain Book Yard when Humphrey and Nora had finished. Books were displayed on tables, shelves sorted neatly and bunting hung from the plastic roof or down the sides of the cases. Nora added a row of flashing pumpkin face lights that Georgina had picked up in a Halloween sale, which Humphrey fitted with new batteries. Humphrey also checked that everything was waterproof as the rain continued to fall, sounding pleasant above them. Then they gave the floor a final sweep.

"I'm so pleased with this." Nora said happily, gazing around the large, bright, airy room now full of bargain books as Humphrey placed the broom in the outside loo.

"Good. I think it will do well."

"I hope so. People were a little bemused at our plans for a Black Friday event in Castletown."

"You get so many tourists that it'll be a hit."

"We do get numerous American visitors too." Nora agreed.

"And everyone's after a bargain book."

"Tell me about it." Nora sighed.

"Georgina worked out that if all these books sell with a fifty percent discount it will bring in ten thousand pounds."

Nora nearly fell into her little pile of sweeping.

"Really?!"

"Yes. And you're only starting on ten percent discount tomorrow so it should be good takings this week."

"Georgina's so confident we will be inundated with bookworm bargain hunters that she has asked Heather to work with Felix and I on Saturday." Nora smiled.

"Sounds fun." Humphrey grinned, wrapped his arms around her and told Nora he was christening the bargain book yard for luck with a smooch.

"Did you know that the Duke of Cole will be abseiling down the largest turret of his castle?" Cara asked Nora as they stood cashing up at the end of the day.

Nora almost dropped a bag of pennies.

"Really?"

"Show off." Humphrey muttered.

"When?"

"At the autumn festival at the castle on Wednesday." Cara read. She was on her iPhone, looking at an e-newsletter from the Castletown events committee.

"In the dark?"

"It will be floodlit."

"Can't wait." Nora grinned.

Humphrey gave her a look.

Once the float had been counted, everything packed away, they had said *'byeeeeeeeee'* to Roger and Betty on the Skype chat, turned off the lights, set the alarm, run out of the shop with Arthur, and huddled under Nora's umbrella because of the rain, Nora locked the door.

"Evening all!"

Cara squealed, Arthur barked and Nora jumped as Seymour stopped behind them. He burst out laughing.

"Did I make you jump?" He grinned.

"Yes!" Cara giggled.

"Seymour!" Nora rebuked her brother.

Humphrey laughed.

"Hey. It's raining. How are we supposed to ice skate?" Seymour asked incredulously after kissing Cara hello.

"The ice rink is in a marquee." Nora explained.

"What about Arthur?"

"He can come." Cara smirked.

"We can take it in turns to sit with him." Nora offered.

They turned left from the bookshop and started to walk towards the river, past the estate agents, across a small road, through a large puddle, past a barber shop, antique centre and post office on the corner, to the ruins of an abbey by the fast flowing waterway. Flashing lights and disco music came from the marquee where people were skating happily inside.

"Connect with nature before winter comes!" Someone bellowed in Nora's ear.

She almost dropped her umbrella.

"Pardon?"

A smiling woman thrust a leaflet under Nora's nose.

"Woodturning, Victorian Christmas wreath making and construct your own corn dolly crafts in Market Street this Saturday. Come along!" The woman demanded.

"Er…thank you." Nora took the leaflet.

"Did you know that the Anglo-Saxons called November *Blotmonap*?" Humphrey asked.

"No." Nora giggled.

"It was known as a month for slaughter." He added.

"Oh. That's not very nice." Nora grimaced.

They entered the ice rink marquee which was large, bright and fresh. Nora did a double take when she saw a familiar face handing out skates behind a long counter. He spotted the bookworm group and his eyes lit up.

"Hiiiiii!" Harry greeted smoothly, grinning stupidly at Nora.

"Terminator alert!" Cara whispered to Nora.

Harry was a local and a regular to The Secondhand Bookworm. He collected Beano and Dandy annuals for his nephew. He was also known as 'The Terminator' because when he had first arrived in town he had been wearing a black tight vest, black jeans, shades and had said to Nora 'I'll be back' just like Arnold Schwarzenegger in the movie. He also fancied Nora, and was especially more doting since she had moved into her flat up the large hill by the top castle gates and was now his neighbour.

"Hello Harry." Nora replied politely.

"Are you working here, Harry?" Humphrey asked.

"Jonas and Kerry from the greengrocers below my flat have organised this, so I'm giving them a hand. What size shoes are you? Let me guess. Nora? A dainty five?"

Nora stared.

"No. A hefty eight." She corrected.

Humphrey and Cara smothered their laughs.

"Oh. Amazing." Harry admired, turning and picking out the correct sized boots.

"I'm an eight too." Cara called.

"Ten." Humphrey said.

"Eleven." Seymour added from where he was crouching down fussing over Arthur and smirked at Humphrey.

While Harry picked out their skates, Humphrey paid Jonas behind the counter.

"We have a discount on British apples and plums. To get into the spirit of the Black Friday week you've bought to Castletown." Jonas told Nora.

"Oh. That's good." She replied.

"You can leave your dog with me." Harry suggested keenly.

"Thanks termina…er, Harry." Cara appreciated.

Seymour walked Arthur around the counter, through a secure gate and passed Harry his lead. While Harry fussed over Arthur, Seymour spotted his younger brother Milton and other sister Heather heading towards them. He waved cheerfully.

"Bookworms!!!" Cara then whispered, nudging Nora's arm.

She looked in the direction that Cara was staring to see two familiar faces on the ice. A man with orange hair that they fondly called The Cat-Man, because he only bought books about cats, was gliding peacefully around the rink while speaking with a tall, blue eyed man who wore what looked like a vampire cape, with a halo of white hair around his head, called Spencer, also a regular at The Secondhand Bookworm. Spencer bought occult books and fancied himself as a medium. Nora and Cara called him the Ghostbuster.

"Bookworms seem to gather everywhere." Nora smirked.

"Hello!" Heather greeted.

"Oh, hi!" Nora grinned. "Hey, Milton."

"Hello." Her brother smiled. Although Milton had never worked at The Secondhand Bookworm, he was familiar with all its ins and outs and enjoyed hearing about any bookworm antics.

Harry was back with the skates.

"Two more please, Harry." Nora smiled.

He smiled keenly back.

"Sure. What sizes?"

"Seven please." Heather replied.

"Ten." Milton nodded.

Humphrey paid for Heather and Milton while Harry fetched more ice skates.

"You can leave any coats, bags and umbrellas with us here, too." Jonas added.

Nora handed over her umbrella and bag.

Before they headed for the rows of wooden benches to put their skates on, Harry asked them what music they would like to skate to.

"Why do we get preference?" Cara asked with a knowing smirk.

"There are six of you in your group." Harry shrugged. "So why not?"

"What are the choices?" Seymour enquired.

"There are lots of themes." Harry explained.

"I most enjoy skating to the sound of ambulance sirens?" Milton joked.

"I enjoy the tunes from ice-cream trucks." Humphrey mused.

"1980's pop songs." Nora requested, slapping Humphrey's arm.

"Grunge music?" Cara piped in.

"Rave music?" Seymour asked.

Heather was giggling too much to make a request.

"1980's pop songs it is." Harry decided.

Everyone groaned.

"Favouritism." Humphrey sighed.

Nora laughed, leading the way to the benches.

They spent five minutes putting on their skates before making their way to the ice-rink. Harry put on the 1980's pop songs. The Secondhand Bookworm group skated with the sound of the rain on the marquee above them and Rick Astley's hit '*never gonna give you up*'.

"Look who it is." Cara gestured as she skated past Nora.

Nora followed the direction of her hand and did a double take.

Drunk-Boy was on the rink without any skates, slipping and sliding with Harry chasing him. He then bent over and vomited.

"FANCY SEEING YOU HERE!" A familiar loud voice hollered.

Nora saw Shouting Stanley leaning on the side of the rink, watching his daughter and two grandchildren.

"Hello." Nora smiled, slowing down as she passed him.

He held up 'Under the Greenwood Tree'.

"I'VE STARTED READING THIS AS I WAIT FOR MY FAMILY. I THINK I'VE FALLEN FOR FANNY AT FIRST SIGHT TOO. DID YOU KNOW THAT HARDY WAS ORIGINALLY GOING TO CALL THE BOOK 'THE MELLSTOCK QUIRE', BUT IN THE END CALLED IT 'UNDER THE GREENWOOD TREE', FROM A LINE IN A SONG IN SHAKESPEARE'S PLAY 'AS YOU LIKE IT'?"

Despite Wham's '*Wake me up before you go-go*' playing extremely loud, everyone in the ice-rink heard Shouting Stanley. His daughter skated up to him really fast.

"DAD! STOP SHOUTING!" She shouted.

"RIGHT YOU ARE!" Shouting Stanley shouted back, winked at Nora and she skated off grinning.

Harry and Jonas were cleaning up Drunk-Boy's vomit. Nora grimaced as she passed it with a wincing Humphrey in tow.

"Nora. Hi."

Nora recognised Alice and her son Grey, both of whom worked at the delicatessen on the corner by The Secondhand Bookworm.

"We're looking forward to your Black Friday book sale week." Alice said.

"Especially your Bargain Book Yard." Grey nodded.

"Are you talking about Black Friday at The Secondhand Bookworm?"

Nora jumped as a middle aged frumpy lady called Miss Raven glided neatly up to her. She stared.

Miss and Mrs Raven were two notorious customers who frequented The Secondhand Bookworm in pursuit of children's books. Miss Raven and her mother argued in whispers and carried a deluge of carrier bags. They demanded discounts and often required several bags for a handful of books.

"Oh. Yes." Nora nodded, staring at Miss Raven's companion. "Is your mother not here?"

"She's over there." Miss Raven indicated distractedly. "Are you going to give us our ten percent discount on any children's books in your Bargain Book Yard?"

"Oh." Nora blinked. "No. I'm afraid not."

"But we are very good, loyal customers." Miss Raven's blue eyes flashed.

"Yes, you are. But the bargain books are already marked specifically down."

"I shall have to speak to Georgina about that!" Miss Raven snapped. "Mother and I will be visiting this week. Come Buford." She addressed the man with her, and they skated off together.

"Wasn't that the man she was with on the beach this summer?" Humphrey asked Nora with a smirk.

"Oh! That's where I recognise him from." Nora realised. She giggled. She then looked over to where Mrs Raven was, buried beneath her enormous pink duffle coat and huge white scarf, and her smile faded. Mrs Raven was glaring at her, puffing.

"I can see that Black Friday at The Secondhand Bookworm is going to be great fun." Nora sighed.

"I'm sure it will." Humphrey assured, took hold of Nora's hand and they skated across the rink amidst the bookworms and flashing strobe lights, accompanied by New Order's appropriately titled 1983 hit '*Blue Monday*'.

3 THE BARGAIN HUNTERS

"Do you stock Lego cards?"

Nora almost dropped the bunch of keys she was holding as she stood opening up The Secondhand Bookworm the following morning. A man loomed up behind her like a spectre.

"Lego cards?"

"Yes. Free ones. They give them away in Sainsbury's." The man persisted.

"I'm afraid not."

"That's a shame. I thought this was a bargain store."

"It's a bookshop. We have a Bargain Book Yard opening today."

"With Lego cards?"

"No."

"Shame. I need Cactus Girl and Fly Monster."

"Oh." Nora looked bemused.

"I'll check next door." He decided and headed off.

Shaking her head, Nora finished opening the door as Betty, her work colleague, arrived.

"Oh, Nora! I almost ran over a duck!" She exclaimed.

"Oh dear." Nora sympathised.

"Flipping things; waddling down the middle of the road without a care in the world. I was reversing into a space along the moat by the castle, trying to get into it before some vicious old greyhead could beat me to the punch, and I heard all this quacking. A mallard ran out from under my car. It was limping a bit but still alive, though I swear it gave me a filthy look. I should have cooked it."

Nora tried not to laugh.

"Thanks for listening." Betty appreciated, closed the door behind them and unzipped her cream gillet as Nora hurried to turn off the alarm.

"Today is Bargain Book Yard day!" Nora announced dramatically.

Betty gave her a look.

"I said to Georgina, are you sure you want to encourage all the pigs asking for discounts. She'll never get rid of them after this." Betty said.

Nora laughed.

"Well, Humphrey said that there would be good profit on all the books from the yard, even when we get to fifty percent off on Black Friday."

"Oh that's alright then." Betty allowed. She gave Nora a curious look. "Are you and Humphrey still together?"

"Oh. Yes." Nora nodded. She cleared her throat. "I tried to break up with him after the Halloween ball at the castle last month. He seemed to still have feelings for his ex-fiancé who is back and whom he danced with at the ball. He also knows I have a crush on the Duke so I said we should just be friends so he could go back to Jenny, who certainly seemed keen on him. But Humphrey insisted he wanted us to stay together and that he's alright with my crush on the Duke and he's not interested in Jenny. So, we're still currently a couple."

Betty pulled a face.

"Humphrey is a handsome devil. And you are so pretty, Nora. You make such a lovely pair. But if the Duke ever asks you to get familiar then throw Humphrey out on his ear." She advised seriously. "I know you're not cohabitating, it's a figure of speech, but the Duke has such lovely legs. Imagine the legs your sons would have."

Nora was still laughing as she filled up the till. She sent Betty off to turn on the upstairs lights and then they both opened up the yard.

"Oh it's beautiful, Nora. What a wonderful job you've done. You're so clever and artistic; you have such an eye for the books and displaying them." Betty praised as Nora turned on the pumpkin face lights.

"Thanks." Nora chuckled. "Although Humphrey did most of the work."

"He was trying to impress you." Betty winked. "But I can see your touch."

They walked around the bright, pleasant Bargain Book Yard, admiring it happily.

"You know it will be wrecked by lunchtime." Nora then said.

"Once the pigs get rummaging." Betty agreed with a scowl.

"It's a shame we have to sell our books." Nora nodded.

They both laughed.

"How about I make us some tea?" Betty suggested.

"Thanks. I'll put some things out on the pavement to encourage customers. It's not raining at the moment."

Nora set off to the front of the shop. She unlocked the door, turned the sign to 'OPEN', changed the number on her poster counting down the days to Black Friday and wheeled the bargain book trolley up the step with lots of huffing and puffing and onto the street as a bright yellow Tuk-Tuk chugged past. Nora did a double take.

The Castletown Tuk-Tuk was relatively new to the town. A spindly man named Karl, with fluffy grey hair and legs like a spider, drove tourists in it about the streets to various destinations around Castletown for a fiver. It had been painted black over Halloween but was now a bright, shiny golden orange, like a tangerine.

"Morning, Gina."

Nora jumped and almost let go of the bargain trolley.

"Oh. Hello." She replied with a polite smile.

Crossword-Lady was standing next to her.

"I don't have a literary question for you for my crossword today." Crossword-Lady said. "But you appear to have lost your touch anyway."

Nora stared.

"Yes, I have." She decided to agree.

"Hopefully you'll get back on your game soon, Gina. You have to be convincing in that new movie role of yours."

"What movie role is that?" Nora asked politely, putting the brakes on the trolley.

"Oh, I read about it in the paper. The new movie called 'The Book Club'. Where they all gather together to read porn." Crossword-Lady replied.

Nora's eyes widened.

"I'm not in that!"

Crossword-Lady smiled knowingly.

"Ah, you're so modest, Gina. But don't worry; your secret is safe with me. I'm off to feed the donkeys now. Goodbye, Gina."

Nora sighed, shaking her head, offended.

Back in the bookshop, Nora noticed a slime trail that seemed to lead from under the Cole bookcase, across the flagstones and the carpet and disappear under the Observer bookcase to the right of the window. A rogue slug had obviously been exploring The Secondhand Bookworm overnight.

"Is your Bargain Book Yard open?" A man's voice hollered into the room.

Nora yelped.

"Oh. Yes. Sorry, you made me jump. Yes, we're open now."

He was short and wore a black Macintosh with a bowler hat. Red hair peeped out from beneath the brim.

"Which way please?" He asked.

"Through there and out into the back." Nora indicated, watching him walk over the slime trail. "All books in the Bargain Book Yard will have ten percent off today."

The man ignored her and headed off.

Nora began to scratch her itchy legs. She glared at the mountains of books piled everywhere.

"Excuse me!" A woman shouted from the doorway.

"Oh. Hello." Nora smiled.

"I was looking at your bargain book trolley and a pigeon did some droppings on my shoulder!"

Nora grimaced.

"I'm sorry about that. We're trying to deal with the problem."

"That does *not* help me now." The woman protested.

"Would you like a wet wipe?"

"No. I would like some compensation." The woman exclaimed.

"Er…well, we can't control the birds outside the shop." Nora said.

"They're sitting on your window ledges up there."

"I can try to shoo them away." Nora offered.

"Forget it! I was going to purchase this book for fifty pence but you can keep it."

Nora watched the woman toss it into the shop where it landed on the slime trail. She then kicked the door frame once with her boot, turned and stomped off, the pigeon poop glistening on her shoulder. For a long moment Nora stared.

"I thought I was going to be molested. But it wasn't my lucky day." Betty's voice interrupted Nora's thoughts.

Nora turned to see Betty arrive with two mugs of tea.

"Who was going to molest you?"

"That handsome man in the bowler hat." Betty smirked.

Nora giggled.

While Betty checked the emails, Nora picked up the discarded book, wiped it free of slug slime on her jeans and returned it to the bargain trolley. She glanced up to see a plump pigeon staring down at her from the bay window, so she smiled at it.

"Oh what a beastly hag!" Betty exclaimed when Nora had returned and told her about the lady with pigeon droppings on her shoulder.

"I agree." Nora nodded, sipping her tea.

"She doesn't deserve our lovely books."

Nora put out the box of free maps next, followed by the black boxes of cheap paperbacks that clipped either side of the door. She examined the sky which looked stormy.

"Yes. Looks like rain later." Albert from the Print Shop located up the hill opposite Nora's flat said. He was taking a morning stroll and returning from the newsagents with his paper. His spaniel was with him, but ignoring Nora because he was distracted by pigeon poop on the pavement.

"Oh, morning Albert."

"Is it worth taking a look at your Bargain Book Yard then?" Albert asked.

"It is." Nora assured, watching Albert's dog. "We have a section out there on wartime subjects."

"I'll try to pop down later then." Albert nodded, gave a wave and set off, dragging his spaniel with him.

Nora pondered the Woman in Gold outside Marbles across the square. She wore a large rain hat and a pink, polka dot rain mac.

"Excuse me."

Nora almost screamed when she turned to face a looming scarecrow.

"Oh! Sorry, I didn't mean to frighten you!"

"That's okay." Nora gasped, clutching her chest.

"Would I be able to leave some flyers with you? They're advertising the 'Spot the Scarecrow' competition that is taking place up in the park by the Duke's folly on Sunday."

Nora took a handful of leaflets.

"Will they be people in scarecrow costumes, like yours?"

"No. Small Scarecrows placed among the parkland trees, the folly, by the lake and the whole area up there." The Scarecrow explained. "It's for a local charity. I hope you can come along. It's good fun."

"Thanks." Nora smiled politely and hastily escaped back into The Secondhand Bookworm.

"Madam? Hey, you there? Madam?"

A woman followed Nora into the shop.

"Hello."

"Where did you get your lovely blouse?" The woman asked.

Nora glanced down.

"Oh, this is my work blouse." She replied, pointing to the embroidered lettering that read 'The Secondhand Bookworm' in blue thread.

"It's lovely. May I purchase one?"

Betty almost choked on her tea.

"Er…we don't sell them." Nora explained. "They're for employees."

"And how would I go about becoming an employee? It's such a lovely blouse."

Nora decided to be firm with the mad woman.

"We don't have any vacancies at the moment."

"Perhaps you can give me the details of your tailor?"

"He immigrated over the summer."

"Is he in Europe?"

"He is."

"I'll seek him out. Cheerio." The woman waved and left.

Nora and Betty stared at one another for a long moment.

"This. Is. A. Mental. Asylum." Nora finally said.

Betty laughed.

"Oh Nora. You handled her wonderfully. For a moment I feared she might tear the blouse from your back."

"It wouldn't surprise me." Nora muttered, returning to her tea.

The morning passed quickly with a growing stream of bargain hunters arriving to explore the Bargain Book Yard. Nora made frequent visits to the yard to check it wasn't being trashed, while selling piles of books with Betty at the counter in between. Anticipation for Black Friday at The Secondhand Bookworm was high, with lots of positive comments.

"It's what this town needs." One man in a white polo neck jumper voiced. "It's good for business to have sales."

Several people quibbled over not receiving a discount on books chosen from about the shop. Nora explained that only books from the Bargain Book Yard would be discounted. This resulted in a few huffs.

"I expected that might happen." Nora grimaced as she and Betty sat down for another round of tea.

"Hmm. And I knew people would want cups of tea if they saw us making one. A fat man placed an order for a cappuccino and called me selfish when I refused to make it for him. I almost shut his head in the fridge."

Nora spluttered on her tea with a laugh.

"It's a shame we can't have another entrance to the yard rather than through the kitchen." Betty pondered. "One woman's ugly son opened the fridge and left the door ajar and the milk was getting warm."

"The cheek!" Nora growled.

"When do we get fifty percent off?" A spotty man asked.

Betty lowered her mug of tea.

"Oh, fifty percent discounts on the books in the Bargain Book Yard will take place on Black Friday." She answered with a glamourous smile.

"Huh. Not today?"

"Ten percent off today." Betty encouraged.

"Huh. How much for cash?" He held up a John Grisham paperback.

"Is it from the Bargain Book Yard?"

The man looked shifty.

"Yeah, sure. Yeah, it is. Sure it is."

Betty was suspicious.

"All of our bargain books are marked in red pencil. So I will take ten percent off of it when you come to pay, *if* it is priced in red pencil."

"What if it's from upstairs?"

"You pay the grey pencil price."

"That's not a bargain."

Betty's lips pursed.

"No. That's the point!"

"I don't see the point of that." Spotty-Man said.

"We have a bargain *yard*." Betty fumed.

"Huh. Well, I didn't find anything I wanted out there. So how much for cash on this?"

Nora decided to step in when she thought she saw steam coming out of Betty's ears.

"I'm sorry sir, but we can only offer ten percent off of books from the Bargain Book Yard."

"Pffft! Rubbish idea." He said, tossed the Grisham at Betty and stomped off.

"Spotty git!" Betty called after him.

Fortunately he didn't hear.

A group of people came from the back, their arms full of books.

"Your kettle doesn't work." A chubby cheeked man said.

"Pardon?" Nora asked.

"I was going to top up my flask of tea and couldn't boil your kettle."

Nora's cheeks flamed.

"You shouldn't be touching anything in the kitchen, sir."

"Keep your hair on." He dumped his pile of books on the counter. "This one is from your train section by the stairs. I assume I'll get ten percent off of it as well as the others from your yard. I'm a bargain hunter."

Betty muttered some insults.

"Sorry. No can do." Nora said loudly.

"Eh? Come on, love. This is a bargain store."

"No. It's not." Nora gritted her teeth. "I can discount all the books from the Bargain Book Yard but not this train book. You will have to pay the full grey pencil price."

"What do you mean, 'full grey pencil price'?" He laughed. "Is that code?"

Nora decided not to answer.

"Do you need a bag, sir?" She smiled schizophrenically.

"Er…yeah, sure, sure." He nodded, staring at Nora warily.

Nora was amazed at how furious she felt as she dealt with the group of bargain hunters. When they had gone she wrote down their sales and looked at Betty who was seething and clicking her teeth.

"I don't see why they can't be happy about the Bargain Book Yard. I feel like burning it to the ground." Nora grumbled.

"Oh don't let them upset you, Nora. They're not worth it." Betty said and made a rude hand gesture at the door just as a woman with her head wrapped in a horrible bright blue scarf appeared.

"Hello Nora! Hello!" A posh, familiar voice greeted.

Nora groaned inside when she saw the Goat-Lady step into the shop.

The Goat-Lady was a local woman who bred rare breeds of farm animals. She lived in a caravan between Castletown and Seatown and liked to buy books about rare breeds of farm animals too, as well as local history guides. Her second husband Bill had a scraggy face and acted lustfully towards Nora.

Nora looked warily behind the Goat-Lady for any sign of Bill. A young man was the only one with her. He was a charcoal burner and his face was black with burned wood. He smiled, showing brilliant white teeth.

"You know Leo." The Goat-Lady gestured.

"Yes. Hello, Leo." Nora nodded.

Leo hurried off to look at the science fiction novels upstairs.

"Anything put by for me, Nora?" The Goat-Lady asked loudly.

Betty curled her lip at the smell of manure.

"Oh. No, not this month."

"We're in town for the sheep racing." The Goat-Lady declared loudly. "I've left Bill speaking with the Duke's gamekeepers. Bill was going to drive one of the pinzgauers on the Deer Rut Safari tonight but he's hurt his arm, the silly man."

Nora breathed a sigh of relief. She didn't fancy being harassed by Bill all evening when she and Humphrey went on the safari.

"Oh dear." Nora sympathised, trying to hide her happy smile. "Did you say 'sheep racing'?"

"Yes. The town events planners approached me about supplying the sheep, but my breeds are rare so I recommended a farmer I know who trains his sheep for racing. It's hilarious fun. They race with teddy bear jockeys on their backs and jump over bales of hay. They'll be closing the road on Saturday for it and the sheep will race down the hill, jumping hay bales, for part of the autumn square dancing and folk festival. Leo will be helping at the betting tent on the cobbles."

Nora and Betty stared.

"That sounds amazing." Nora laughed.

"Oh, it is, Nora! Are you related to gypsies?"

Nora blinked.

"Erm…"

"As you know, I'm related to Matthew Hopkins, the Witch Finder General, so I have an eye for people with gifts. You look like you could detect a witch or too, Nora."

"Oh she can." Betty agreed with a look.

Nora smirked.

Leo reappeared.

"Nothing today, mum." He said.

"Alright. Let's go and find Bill then." The Goat-Lady decided.

"Hello gorgeous!" Bill had appeared in the doorway and was grinning at Nora.

Nora's smile faded.

"Leave her alone, Bill." The Goat-Lady rebuked, heading for the door.

"See you again soon, gorgeous." Bill winked and they left.

"What an awful man. You should set Humphrey on him, Nora." Betty glowered.

Nora sprayed air freshener around once they had gone.

"I think I'd like some lunch now." She sighed, coughing slightly because of the lavender smell.

"Oh, go ahead, Nora. I'll hold the fort here." Betty assured.

"Thanks. I'll go to the secret garden down River Road. It's not raining and I could do with some fresh air." She decided, grabbing her bag.

"That sounds lovely, Nora. Have a nice time." Betty smiled.

"Good luck with the bargain hunters." Nora hoped.

Betty scowled but then smiled, waved goodbye and Nora set off from The Secondhand Bookworm for a break!

4 THE DEER RUT SAFARI

The secret garden was a public garden on the banks of the river, nestled between two three-story houses down a winding road not far from the town square. It was known only to locals and was a quiet place for shop workers to eat a peaceful lunch. Tourists only discovered it rarely, and when they did they were soon chased away by glares, scowls, and frowns from the locals.

"Nora!" A familiar voice hailed as she closed the wooden gate behind her.

Nora turned to see Charles, Tobey and Imogen sitting on the benches that circled a tall tree in the middle of the garden.

Charles was waving at her, beckoning Nora join them.

"Afternoon." Nora smiled.

Imogen shuffled up to make room for Nora.

"Long time, no see." She greeted and offered Nora an organic apple from a batch she had brought with her from her organic greengrocer shop.

"Thanks." Nora appreciated.

"We were just talking about your Black Friday endeavour." Tobey, who worked in the bank, revealed.

Nora placed her baguette on her lap, followed by a bag of crisps, chocolate bar, the organic apple and a steaming coffee; the latter she placed next to her.

"Really? What do you think?"

"Very good idea." Charles nodded. A regular at The Secondhand Bookworm, Charles was a serious book collector. He had blond hair and always wore a pinstriped suit with cufflinks.

"Are you looking for book bargains, Charles?" Nora smiled.

Charles shook his head.

"No. You know I like to read original publications and bindings. A couple of work colleagues are interested in your book sale though. They were talking about it in the office."

"Great." Nora nodded and took an enormous bite of her sandwich, still fuming about the bargain hunters.

"I expect everyone's asking for a discount." Tobey said knowingly.

"Hmm. I get the feeling it's going to be a lot of hard work this week." Nora sighed through her mouthful.

A crow landed in front of them. They all stared at it. It stared back. It then cawed threateningly so Nora threw a bit of her baguette for it. Three seagulls noticed so swooped noisily down to join the crow. There was a large fight with feathers and shrieks, much to Charles and Tobey's amusement. In the end, a rook stole the piece of baguette that had been discarded in the crow and seagull fight, so Nora had to throw some more to placate the angry crow, which looked pleased, picked it up and flew off quickly with the screaming seagulls chasing it.

"That's enough entertainment for me." Tobey laughed, standing up.

"Yes, I'd better get back to the office, too." Charles agreed.

Nora and Imogen bade them goodbye.

"Uh-oh." Imogen smirked.

The crow had returned. Nora sighed.

"I can see I shall be doing this until I've eaten everything." She said.

"You have a way with animals." Imogen grinned.

They chatted about books and vegetables while feeding the crow and seagulls, until a swan appeared on the wall beside the river bank and eyed Nora's crisps while hissing. Nora and Imogen made a run for it.

"They reminded me of the bargain book hunters." Nora told Imogen as they walked along River Road.

Imogen laughed.

"People ask for money off fruit and vegetables too."

"You're joking!"

"No. It's annoying." Imogen empathised.

"That makes me feel better."

"Share the pain." Imogen grinned, bade Nora goodbye and they parted by the Traditional Sweetshop.

Nora was peering at the sweets in the window display when she heard a crow cawing, so decided to hurry back to The Secondhand Bookworm.

"*A reminder for everyone to please dress smart for Thursday's Thanksgiving dinner. Looking forward to having you all. Large kiss, small kiss, small kiss.*" Betty read, scrolling down a text message on her phone that both she and Nora had received from Georgina when Betty had returned from her lunch.

Nora chuckled.

"Oh Nora. I'm so glad Georgina didn't ask us to bring a plus one. That wretched grey-head I've been dating, Marvin, won't leave me alone."

"Marvin? I've never heard of him." Nora smirked, polishing the till.

"Oh haven't I told you about him, Nora? How remiss of me!" Betty's eyes twinkled. She lowered her mobile. "My daughters hate him. We met online and he's a devilish man. He told me he didn't smoke but on our first date I could smell cigarettes on him. When he swooped in to kiss me his breath was like mint and fags. I almost heaved. And his hands, they're like an octopus's Nora, all over my body, in the street outside the restaurant, and I admit it was rather thrilling at first, but I was fed up of it by morning."

Nora looked scandalized. Betty grinned.

"I think I've heard enough." Nora said.

"Well, I'd *had* enough. He left his y-fronts and his false teeth at my house on purpose and kept sending me erotic text messages. In the end I told him to clear off but he stalks me on Facebook and if he hears I'm going out for a meal he will insist on coming."

Nora was laughing.

"Oh dear." She sympathised.

"Dirty grey-head." Betty insulted, though she looked pleased at having a stalker.

"Hello!" A man in a fur coat emerged from the back of the shop, carrying armfuls of bargain books. He had silver hair, swept back like The Fonz.

"Hello." Nora smiled, warily.

"Am I right in thinking I get fifty percent off of these?" He asked.

Nora inwardly groaned.

"I'm afraid not. It's ten percent off today."

"Oh." He frowned. "Okay then."

He placed them on the counter and rummaged in his coat for his wallet.

Nora spotted several in the pile that she knew were not from the Bargain Book Yard. She siphoned them out.

"These are from the history section. I can't offer a discount on them." She said.

The man paused.

"This is supposed to be a bargain book shop."

"No. The books in the Bargain Book Yard are discounted." Nora explained.

Betty attempted to smile glamorously at the man.

"But all of our books are lovely and marked at such a good value." Betty assured.

The man ignored her.

"That's false advertising. I came in here expecting a book sale."

"There is a book sale." Nora said, feeling the tips of her ears getting hotter.

"It doesn't sound like it to me. It sounds like a bit of a scam, luring people into your shop and picking and choosing which books to discount."

"I'll put them back on the shelves then, sir." Nora decided.

"Hold up!" He lunged for them and covered the pile with his large, sweaty palms.

Nora and Betty stared.

The man stared.

It was a stand-off.

"Fine!" He finally relented and took out a large, leather wallet. "I'll take them anyway."

Warily, Nora opened each book for Betty to read and punch the price into the till. She put the books marked with red pencil through first, did a ten percent discount and then ran the prices of the history books through, finally pressing total. The man 'humphed' at that but handed over a pile of cash. Betty gave him his change, still smiling glamorously.

"Bag?" He asked Betty.

Betty unhooked a plastic blue bag, she and Nora placed the books inside, and Nora passed it to him.

"Thanks." The man said, glared at Betty and stomped off.

Once he was gone, Betty's smile became a snarl.

"What an old…" She began but another costumer arrived so she stopped in mid insult.

"Hello. Do you have a copy of 'Red and the Pumpkins'?" The lady asked.

"Oh! As in 'Red' from the Fraggle Rock television programme in the 1980's?" Nora asked, excited.

The woman grinned.

"Yes! I love anything to do with Red. The story is great. Red finds a pumpkin seed so decides to plant it because it would be less dangerous for the Fraggles to grow their own food rather than steal dangerously from the Gorgs. But the pumpkins take over Fraggle Rock. It was published in 1983."

"I'm afraid I haven't seen it." Nora said. "And I would remember it because I would have read it."

"Oh that's a shame. I also collect anything about Rainbow Brite. Look at my t-shirt!"

With a loud popping sound, the woman tore open her coat to reveal a retro t-shirt. Nora and Betty stared.

"I have the German edition of 'Red and the Pumpkins'. It's called 'Red und die Kürbisse', also published in 1983. In addition I have the Finnish, 'Red ja kurpitsat' and the French 'Mag et les citrouilles', as well as the Swedish 'Vips og pumporna'; they were published in 1984. But I look in every secondhand bookshop I come by for the English version."

Nora was trying her hardest not to laugh at the foreign translations.

"Well hopefully one day you will come across it. Would you like me to look on any secondhand book websites for you?" She tittered.

"No, that's okay. I like the thrill of the hunt!" The woman said, doing up her coat. "Great shop. And awesome Bargain Book Yard. Bye!"

Nora felt better having dealt with the eccentric woman and her positive attitude.

She felt even better when Betty made them a round of tea and got out two large wedges of carrot cake.

"My daughter made this for me. It was an enormous cake. I think she wants me to have a heart attack so she can inherit my bungalow."

Nora laughed as she bit into her slice.

At four o'clock, Humphrey arrived. He looked handsome in his blue woollen sweater, black jeans, boots and cap.

"We're set for the Deer Rut tonight." He announced happily, leaning into Nora and kissing her.

Betty smirked, thoughtfully.

"Great."

"I thought we could go to The Duke's Pie for a bite to eat afterwards. The safari starts at dusk so we'll need to get going at five o'clock sharp." He explained.

"I can lock up, Nora." Betty offered generously. "You can leave early."

Humphrey looked pleased.

"I couldn't possibly leave you with all these *mad* bargain hunters." Nora told Betty in a low voice as one man wearing a onesie strolled past, heading for the Bargain Book Yard.

"I insist!" Betty said. "If anyone gives me trouble I'll glare at them. Like this!"

She glowered menacingly. Nora agreed that would frighten anyone off.

"Alright." Nora laughed. "Thank you."

"Excuse me." A large woman emerged through the walkway into the back room, carrying a list.

"Hello." Betty smiled politely.

"I'll go down to the corner shop and buy us some drinks and snacks." Humphrey said, leaning in to kiss Nora again.

"Okay, thanks." Nora smiled. She turned to survey the customer.

"I'm looking for two specific books about cheese-making but you don't have anything in your book yard."

"Cheese making is quite a specific subject. It's unlikely we would have discounted any books about it." Nora piped in.

The woman's chubby face fell.

"I specifically want a bargain!" She announced.

Betty cleared her throat.

"Have you looked upstairs?"

"Are the books up there discounted?"

"Well…no."

"Then NO I haven't." The cheese lady exclaimed, lifted her chin and stormed off clutching her list.

Two ladies carrying postcards entered after she had left.

"Do you have any postcards of the Castletown ducks?" One lady asked.

"Is that the local football team?" Betty asked.

Nora suppressed a laugh. The woman looked confused.

"The ducks down at the lake." The woman explained.

"Shut my mouth." Betty muttered to the woman before flashing a dazzling smile. "I'm sorry, the only designs we have are the ones on the postcard spinners outside."

"Oh." The woman dumped a large knitted bag onto the counter. "Do you sell stamps?"

"We do!" Betty assured enthusiastically.

The sound of a trumpet fanfare from the computer announced the arrival of a Skype message from Seatown so Nora hastily turned to read it.

'Greetings fellow Zorgs. Do you have the Star Trek the Next Generation graphic novel: Star Trek TNG: Mirror Broken? By Scott Tipton (Author), David Tipton (Author) and J. K. Woodward (Artist). Customer waiting (hurry because he is a nerd!) – Cara xxx'

Nora smirked.

'Rather specific but you never know. Will have a look.'

'Thanks. I sorted out a large Star Trek section in the paperback room. There could be some graphic novels left.'

'Ok'

Nora told Betty she was running upstairs. Betty waved her off with a pair of scissors as she stood cutting out stamps from a small book of six for one of the women. The other stopped Nora.

"I'm staying on a static caravan site. It's awful." She shared desperately. "The walls are paper thin. You can hear the people in the other caravans fart. On the left side there's a family like hillbillies. One boy stands hitting a swing-ball while wearing boxing gloves until eight in the evening. And it seems like they sell their caravans. It's like a goblin town with decking and gardens added to every other one."

Nora's eyes widened.

"Oh dear." She sympathised.

"I can't wait to leave. So much for a November holiday. These please." She handed Nora some paperbacks from the bargain trolley outside.

"Oh. Can I ask my colleague to serve you these as there is only one till and I need to look for a book upstairs?"

"There's a queue." The woman pointed to the lady she had entered with.

"I'm sure that lady won't be long."

"It's my sister and she doesn't shut up. I'll let one go and that'll hurry her along." The woman decided, taking back the books.

Nora decided to flee the scene. She was soon running up the stairs to the attic room where the paperbacks were stocked.

The paperback room was a converted attic so the ceilings were sloped all around and there was a double window that overlooked the yard. Nora headed straight for the window. As she stood before it, scratching her itchy legs, she smiled at the abundance of plastic roofing Humphrey had erected over the entire area. It was presently clean, although a few large red bird droppings had splattered on some areas. Nora supposed the culprit had been eating berries. She could see strange forms through the frosted roof, rummaging through the Bargain Book Yard and sighed happily at the fantasy of bookselling. She then turned and headed for the science fiction section behind her but stopped dead in her tracks.

A large space on the wall above the fantasy section greeted her. Nora looked wildly around, checked the other walls and then dug out her iPhone. As she knelt before the Star Trek books, she dialled Cara's mobile.

"Hi!" Cara greeted cheerfully.

"I'm in the paperback room." Nora said.

"Any luck?"

"Oh. No I'm still looking. But I wanted to ask if you or anyone else had moved the large poster we had on the wall of the map of Middle Earth."

Cara paused.

"No. Is it missing?"

"I can't see it anywhere."

"OMGosh! Someone must have stolen it." Cara exclaimed. "Sorry, Arthur."

Nora sat back on her haunches.

"That was my first thought. The cheek!"

"I can't believe it. How horrible."

"I bought that in Oxford, especially for the paperback room." Nora glowered.

"I did suggest that Humphrey use wallpaper paste to fix it to the wall. But Georgina didn't agree."

"Hmm. I'd better check the children's room. I put some lovely Narnia postcards around from C. S Lewis' book illustrations." Nora mused.

The distant sound of a school bell ringing drew her attention.

"Oh. I forgot to bring up a walkie-talkie. Betty's ringing the school bell." Nora realised, standing up. "No luck with the Star Trek graphic novel."

"Ok. Thanks for looking."

Nora began down the stairs. The sound of the bell ringing grew louder.

"I can hear that." Cara giggled.

"I'm coming!" Nora called to Betty.

The ringing abruptly stopped.

"I'd better go. A mad man is approaching with books from the bargain yard." Cara informed Nora.

"How's it going with the bargain yard there? The bargain hunters are driving me crazy here." Nora said.

"Roger almost had two fights."

Nora burst out laughing.

"He's a Buddhist."

"Yes, I told him Buddhists are supposed to be gentle people. He was really annoyed with me. I'll tell you about it later."

"Ok. Bye." Nora grinned and hung up as she reached the bottom of the stairs.

In the front room, Betty was still holding the bell. Two men were at the counter. Betty gave Nora a look.

"I was explaining to these gentlemen that we can only give ten percent off of the books from the Bargain Book Yard. They insisted on speaking with the manager. Sorry, Nora." Betty explained.

"No problem." Nora smiled and stopped behind the counter.

The two men were glaring at her. One was very thin and covered in moles. His companion was thicker set, with a neck like a tree trunk.

"Yes, as my colleague said, we can only discount…" Nora began but was interrupted.

"This book is marked too high. How much for cash?" Mole-Man demanded.

Nora looked at the book.

"It makes no difference to us if you pay cash or by card. Actually, scrap that. It's better for us if you pay by card." Nora replied.

"I'm actually negotiating for a bargain." Mole-Man said.

"Yeah!" Tree-Trunk-Neck joined in.

Nora thought he looked like an Ent.

"I'm sorry. The prices are fixed." She assured.

"That's not the spirit of Black Friday." Mole-Man glowered.

Nora paused. The book he was having a tantrum about had actually sat on the shelves for a long time. Nora had debated about adding it to the Bargain Book Yard but changed her mind. It was a large book about playing golf and was very boring.

"Look. In the spirit of Black Friday, I would be happy to reduce the price by a pound." She decided.

Mole-Man pondered that for a moment.

"Take it!" Tree-Trunk-Neck encouraged.

"I shall." Mole-Man nodded, triumphantly.

Both men's hostility deflated.

"Thank you. I like a good bargain." Mole-Man smiled, taking out a leather wallet.

Nora smiled politely and left Betty to run the sale through the till as Humphrey returned. He was carrying a bag of snacks and drinks as well as four free-standing air fresheners and some more flea powder. A man was rummaging through the large piles of books in front of the window. Nora considered throwing flea powder over him.

"Thank goodness. My legs are still itching like crazy."

"No problem." Humphrey grinned.

They left Betty with the men, who were now flirting with her, and took the air fresheners into the Bargain Book Yard, which had the faint smell of cigarette smoke from the Indian restaurant windows. Nora tutted.

"We'll put them on the tops of the cases." Humphrey decided.

A woman turned around from where she was reading a book beside a table.

"A pigeon did a large poop on the roof. Look up there." She told Nora.

Nora looked up.

"Oh dear."

"Can't say I'm looking forward to dismantling this next week." Humphrey muttered.

"Mmm, cinnamon." Nora sniffed, opening the air fresheners.

"I thought I would go for food or spice related fragrances. I have berry and citrus."

"It'll smell like a cake shop out here." Nora grinned.

Humphrey was taller than Nora so he placed the air fresheners around. Nora then spent some time having a tidy up, amazed at how many gaps there were on the shelves already. She told Humphrey about the stolen map of Middle Earth and so they checked the children's room, pleased to see the Narnia postcards were still there.

"I'll paste them to the wall." Humphrey decided.

Nora agreed.

At half past four, Betty insisted that Nora head off with Humphrey for the Deer Rut Safari.

"Just think of all those pheromones in the air this evening." Betty told Nora as Humphrey popped upstairs to the loo after having brought the cheap paperback boxes, bargain book trolley, free maps and postcard spinners inside. "Humphrey might get ideas."

"Shhh." Nora giggled.

"Would that be a bad thing?"

"Yes."

"You shouldn't be with him if you're not in love with him." Betty advised. "I speak from experience. I was with Greg, a grey-headed letch, for one year and he made me feel sick every time he kissed me. I was pleased when I finally cast him off."

"Humphrey doesn't make me sick." Nora assured with a laugh.

"But your heart belongs to someone else." Betty sighed, dreamily.

Nora smiled, shrugging into her coat.

"I enjoy spending time with Humphrey. We have fun."

"But by keeping him as a boyfriend you could be stopping your dreams come true." Betty reminded Nora, hinting at Castletown's most famous, royal resident.

Nora wouldn't allow herself to think about the Duke of Cole too much. She was sure plenty of ladies had a crush on him.

Humphrey returned, typing on his iPhone.

"Ready to go?" He asked, shoving the phone into his pocket.

"Ready." Nora nodded, giving Betty a look.

Betty smiled.

"Have a lovely time. Among the pheromones." She bade.

Humphrey laughed.

"You discovered my motives." He joked, winking at Betty.

"Handsome devil." Betty sighed. "If only I was fifty years younger."

Laughing, Humphrey and Nora bade goodbye and left The Secondhand Bookworm, heading off into the dusk. As they stepped outside, the bright yellow Tuk-Tuk pulled up next to them at the kerb.

"Need a lift anywhere, Nora?" Karl asked cheerfully.

Nora and Humphrey looked at one another.

"Do you have a mind-reading beacon on that?" Humphrey asked.

Karl smiled.

"I just gave a couple a lift up to the park gates. Spike told me you two had booked the Deer Rut Safari." He confessed.

"Great business acumen." Nora admired.

"We can't say no." Humphrey grinned.

Nora agreed.

"How much?"

"Five pounds." Karl replied.

Nora chuckled.

Humphrey dug out his wallet and handed Karl a five pound note. He and Nora then climbed into the back of the Tuk-Tuk, settled back comfortably and Karl put his foot down, driving them down to the mini roundabout, turning back into the town and taking them on an enjoyable journey up the steep hills of Castletown to the Duke's park.

In the parklands of the Duke of Cole's estate, past the folly tower that overlooked the lake, and along a winding path into the hills, a series of large wooden cabins welcomed safari goers with hot drinks and a video about the Duke's rewilding project as the sun began to set.

Nora and Humphrey sat together on wooden chairs as Spike, one of the gamekeepers, introduced the film and stood texting as it played for the group of twenty eight people. They learned about conventional nature conservation and using natural water courses and grazing animals to increase wildlife and care for the land.

Spike then gave a talk about the deer and held up antlers.

"They're the largest in the world." He said.

When everyone was ready, they climbed aboard the Pinzgauers, which Humphrey explained to Nora were Austrian troop carriers. The vehicles then set off into the wilds. The tracks were wild and rough, with plenty of bumps.

Nora was delighted when they spotted a little owl and several large pigs.

The Pinzgauers bounced to a specific site. Holding hands, Nora and Humphrey climbed out of their vehicle and gathered around Spike who told everyone that the lekking grounds were over there and they would get good views up in the tree platforms.

"This is awesome." Nora told Humphrey, snuggling close to him as they hiked along the track.

"I agree." He smiled.

The sounds of roars, from mature deer defending the doe from younger bucks, could be heard. The group climbed tree platforms into enormous oaks and were able to see the spectacular sights.

Clashing antlers echoed about the dusky fields. Nora and Humphrey watched as Spike pointed out two bucks parallel walking and then engaging in a battle.

Nora's thoughts were filled with esteem for the Duke as she admired his land. It was beautiful and wild, natural and breath-taking, where the animals roamed free and were the kings of the land.

Darkness fell and the deer retreated into their sleeping areas. The groups climbed down from the tree platforms and boarded the Pinzgauers where they were taken to a stunning area by a lake to watch owls gliding slowly over the water. Spike and the two Pinzgauer drivers cooked a mixture of vegetarian and venison sausages, which Humphrey and Nora devoured, washed down with sloe gin and hot chocolate spiced with cinnamon and nutmeg.

"Thank you for an incredible evening." Nora said as she and Humphrey stood on the doorstep of her flat.

Castletown was lively, with people arriving at the pubs and restaurants. They had managed to fit in a meal at The Duke's Pie after returning from the safari and now Nora was yawning behind her hands.

"Have a good sleep." Humphrey said, kissing the top of her head.

"I had a lovely time." Nora smiled.

"Me too."

It looked as though Humphrey wished to say something, but changed his mind. He gave her another kiss, and a tight hug, before heading off.

Nora watched him go, her thoughts on Deacon Victor turning to crime as she planned to finish volume four of her detective mystery novel after an exhausting bookshop day!

5 BELLEROPHON BOOKS

Heavy rain bombarded the windows of The Secondhand Bookworm the following morning and the wind blew hard, rattling the blind against the wall above the bay window. Nora reeled it in using a large hook and pole that was kept in the rafters of the front room. When she returned inside she was soaked.

"Oh dear. You look rather wet." Paperback Pam pointed out as she arrived and stepped into the shop.

"Morning. Yes, I am rather." Nora smiled.

"Shall I make you a nice cup of tea?" Paperback Pam offered.

She stood in the doorway shaking out her umbrella over Hugh the street cleaner who happened to be walking past. Hugh glared in affront but was preoccupied with his mission to place cones around enormous puddles at the bottom of the bridge, so hurried off without rebuking her.

"That would be lovely." Nora said, rubbing paper towels over her head.

They turned on the heater behind the desk. Nora hung her parka on a handle for an overhead cupboard above the alarm pad and soon she and her clothes were drying out.

While Paperback Pam made tea, Nora set up for the day, turned the door sign to 'OPEN', changed the number in her countdown to Black Friday poster, stuck up a sign saying '20% off all books in The Bargain Book Yard today!' and checked the emails. Paperback Pam returned with two steaming mugs of very milky tea. After taking a sip, Nora took the keys and unlocked the kitchen door, opening up the Bargain Book Yard.

The rain sounded like bullets on the plastic roofing above. Inside, the yard was cosy and smelt incredible. Spices, fruits and hints of flowers laced the air. Nora smiled triumphantly at the bookcases behind which the smokers' window was located. She checked the area for leaks but everything was perfectly dry. She then jumped.

"There's a man here wishing to speak with the owner." Paperback Pam said.

She stood in the kitchen doorway, admiring the Bargain Book Yard.

"Okay. I'll come through."

"Do you need me to sort out these paperbacks?" Paperback Pam asked.

"I think they're perfectly sorted." Nora replied.

"Okay. Well, I'll disappear upstairs and get to work sorting out the attic room."

Nora glanced back over her shoulder.

"Oh. Okay. Can you take a walkie-talkie up in case I get swamped with customers?" She asked.

Paperback Pam looked reluctant.

"Alright."

They both returned to the front of the shop.

A man with huge black, curly hair, large black glasses, a check shirt and black tie stood waiting patiently at the counter. He looked to be in his early thirties.

"Hello. I'm from Bellerophon Books." The man said.

Nora stared. She then gasped.

"OH! Finally!" She exclaimed, making Paperback Pam flinch.

The man laughed.

"I'm Clive."

"Nora." Nora said, staring at him thoughtfully.

Paperback Pam picked up the walkie-talkies. Nora noticed.

"Can you bear with me a moment, Clive?" She asked.

"Sure." Clive smiled.

Nora fiddled with the devices, changing channels when a man's voice announced loudly: "OLD MAN AT WINDMILL ROAD!"

"Taxis." She told a shocked Paperback Pam.

When the walkie-talkies had finally chosen a peaceful channel, Nora passed one to paperback Pam.

"I'll be back down for lunch." Paperback Pam said and headed off.

Nora stared after her, disgruntled.

"I'm sorry I haven't visited before." Clive said.

Nora turned back to him.

"I wish you had." She grinned. "We've been confused about the mysterious Bellerophon Bookshop for years."

Nora had been baffled when several customers over many years had asked if The Secondhand Bookworm was actually called Bellerophon Books and sold on the internet? She had never been able to discover a second bookshop in Castletown and had had no luck even finding them online.

"I can't believe people have come to town looking for us. We specify that we only sell online."

"I couldn't even find you online." Nora admitted.

"We're on the Dark Web."

Nora stared.

"Just kidding." Clive grinned.

"I thought for a moment you sold manuals for hitmen or how to make bombs." Nora said.

Clive laughed.

"No. But we are on the *deep* web and people have to have special software and a password to access our online site and online catalogue. We don't come up in search engines because we like to trade through book fairs, mainly comic cons, and make ourselves known face to face. We keep a specific, choice clientele."

"Oh. Fair enough." Nora smiled.

"If you get asked again, please, feel free to give the enquirer my card. I'm located at the end of Market Street and all my books are stored there. Occasionally I allow people to visit, and if someone has made the effort to seek me out then I accept that they're serious buyers."

Nora took a small pile of business cards from Clive.

"Perhaps you would like a tour one day yourself?" He added, hopefully.

Nora smiled politely.

"Thank you."

"Great shop. Mind if I have a look around? I've never been in before. Crazy isn't it?"

"Go ahead." Nora nodded and watched him head off through the walkway into the back of the shop. She studied the cards warily. They had a mythical font for 'Bellerophon Books' on the top, followed by Clive's full name, which was Clive Greenburg, and then his mobile number. Nothing else. Nora thought he seemed a bit suspicious with his deep web enterprise and didn't like the idea of sending people off to his secret lair, so she placed the cards in her plastic file that was kept under the counter.

A trumpet sounded, heralding the arrival of a Skype message.

'Morning! How was the deer rut? Betty says you won't break up with Humphrey! – Cara xxx'

Nora's eyes widened. She then smirked.

'Morning! Deer rut was amazing. Humphrey and I are happy!'

Nora watched the pen start moving.

'You don't lurve him. And what about His Grace?'

'I haven't seen His Grace for a while.'

'Well this will help. The third Jeeves and Wooster just came in for sale and I bought it! Nice condition, no wrapper, bright, fresh copy, orange cloth with black lettering, published by Herbert Jenkins Limited, 1930. Georgina told me to price it at two hundred pounds. It's called 'Very good, Jeeves'.'

Nora's heart leaped.

She had been collecting first edition copies of the Jeeves and Wooster books by P. G. Wodehouse for the Duke ever since she had given him the first book in the series as a thank you present for giving her a private tour of his library. When she had learned his valet was named Jeeves she had been delighted. The Duke was now a keen collector and was eagerly awaiting book three.

'Can you send it over here?! He'll have it!!!'

'LOL.' Cara replied. *'I'll bring it over tonight. You can tell him about it at the festival if you see him.'*

'Oh I doubt I'll see him.' Nora wrote with a sigh.

'You never know xxxx' Cara sent back.

Nora smiled.

Her thoughts drifted to the Duke of Cole, a tall, enigmatic recluse. Although a handsome, eligible bachelor at thirty two, the media rarely reported on him, since he had always kept to himself and was never seen at any royal functions or parties. He ran an architectural enterprise and was known for excellent collections of art and furniture, but he was considered boring having lived in an estate on the border of Scotland most of his life, like James Bond's house in Skyfall, and there was never any gossip to be reported upon relating to him. The largest story about him so far, after he had built his new castle, was that he was going to abseil down one of his castle turrets.

Nora knew that the Duke had moved down from his estates near Scotland and in Norfolk to reside in his new, large, renovated castle that overlooked Castletown because it was hidden quietly among the Cole hills and afforded him peace and quiet with his books.

Nora and the Duke of Cole had struck up a friendship last Christmas and after several meetings, Nora was patiently awaiting spending time with him again at her Book Club, even if it would be with several other people. She had resisted sending him a text to see how he was and had been quietly waiting to catch a glimpse of him at the Autumn Festival in the castle, even if it was from afar. She had missed not seeing him since Halloween.

Impulsively, she took out her phone, pausing thoughtfully to watch the typhoon that seemed to be occurring out in the streets.

The rain pelted the windows and a beefy man ran past chasing a poppy that had blown off the front of his coat. The Secondhand Bookworm was quiet and empty, the town seemingly abandoned. It reminded Nora of the first time she had met the Duke over Christmas. The town had been abandoned then, but because of snow rather than rain.

Caught up in her dreamy memories, Nora decided to send the Duke a polite text.

'Hello, Your Grace. Hoping all is well with you.' She typed carefully.

The door flew open and Nora almost dropped her phone.

"Flipping heck! It's like a tsunami out there!" A man hollered, scrambling inside and dripping on the flagstones.

Nora stared.

"Morning." She smiled sympathetically.

"I saw your poster about the Bargain Book Yard. Which way please?" The man asked.

"Through to the back." Nora pointed, cringing at the water dripping from him.

He stomped over the carpet, leaving shoe shaped wet prints, squeezed through the walkway and popped out into the stairwell.

"In the back through the kitchen." She called after him.

"Right you are."

Nora ignored the wet everywhere and sat back down to her phone.

'We have acquired book three of the Jeeves and Wooster series. It is called 'Very good, Jeeves' and was published in 1930. I haven't seen it yet but it is supposed to be very fine – Nora.'

Nora reread the message serval times, bit her cheek and pressed send.

She had just placed her phone onto the shelf beneath the counter when she heard a text message alert. She almost fell off the swivel chair when she grabbed it.

'Nora, I'm so pleased to hear from you. How are things with Humphrey? That is wonderful about the 'Very good, Jeeves' book. When can I come to buy it? Are you coming to the festival tonight? James.'

Nora stared.

Her thumb was shaking so she spelled several words wrong in her reply and spent an extra minute correcting them.

'Yes, of course I'm coming to the festival tonight. How could I pass up the opportunity to watch an abseiling Duke? The book will be here tomorrow. Nora.'

She pressed send, her heart racing.

A moment later:

'Nora, I am so pleased you are coming tonight. Can we arrange for me to view and purchase the book?'

She swallowed hard.

'Of course. When are you free?'

'I am always free for you, Nora. Would tomorrow lunchtime suit? I would like you to taste a batch of pumpkin cakes my cook made me. You will love them.'

Nora grinned.

'I would like that very much. Tomorrow it is. Would you like to come to my flat at one o'clock? I think the garden will be a bit too wet!'

'Nora, nothing would give me greater pleasure. I hope to see you tonight.'

'See you tonight' Nora grinned.

She had just put her phone down when another message arrived from the Duke. It just said:

'Humphrey?'

Nora's mouth went dry. She remembered a conversation she had had with the Duke in his library the night of his Halloween Ball, when she had thought he had been hinting at his romantic interest in her, and that if she didn't have true feelings for Humphrey she should let Humphrey know. She had since convinced herself that she had imagined the Duke would actually be interested in her, and when Humphrey had insisted they remain together, she had remained with him as a couple even though she had told him she held a torch for the Duke of Cole. Now her cheeks flamed.

Clive returned with a pile of books.

"What a treasure trove. Mind if I start a pile? There are some great books that my specialist clientele will be interested in." He said.

"Of course." Nora smiled.

"I stock books about modern day hippie, hippie subcultures, Bohemian, Free Spirit, also science fiction and fantasy." Clive explained.

"We have a great sci-fi and fantasy section on the top floor."

"Oh I shall have a look!" He said and set off.

Nora looked down at her phone. She pondered it for a long time and then typed a message,

'That's a long story' Nora finally sent.

She chewed her bottom lip, waiting. A message finally came.

'I look forward to hearing it. See you soon. James'

Nora smiled. She then sat thinking about Humphrey.

The morning passed slowly, with constant rain and very few customers. Nora called Paperback Pam down so she could run to the toilet. She then made them both tea and Paperback Pam took hers upstairs to continue tidying the paperback room. Nora sighed.

Finally, towards lunchtime, the rain stopped. The clouds cleared, the sun came out and Nora spent five minutes hoisting all the outside objects onto the street. The traffic picked up, people emerged and arrived and Hugh whizzed around on a machine sucking up puddles.

Clive from Bellerophon Books was still searching for books. He had come down three more times with several piles so Nora had grabbed an empty box to put them all in from under the stairs, screamed loudly as a large spider had run towards her, covered it with the bin and asked Paperback Pam to remove it.

Paperback Pam reluctantly came downstairs, picked up the spider and placed it in a puddle on the street.

"When are you going to have lunch, Nora?" Paperback Pam asked.

Nora noticed the time.

"Are you hungry?" She asked.

"No, but I could do with a cigarette break."

"Oh. Do you smoke?"

"Didn't your mum tell you?"

"No."

"I used to always take cigarette breaks when I worked with your mum at the school. The stress of being a bursar. I'm glad I retired."

"Well, if you would like one now go ahead."

"That would be nice. Thank you." Paperback Pam nodded and picked up her handbag. "I shall go to the middle of the square and read the names on the war memorial."

"Okay." Nora nodded, bemused.

Clive reappeared.

"You have some good mythology books. I also specialize in them, hence the name of my book service."

"Of course." Nora said politely, watching him curiously.

"Oh, a box. Thank you. Back I go."

"Would you like a drink?" Nora felt she should ask him.

He looked at his watch.

"Cripes. Is that the time. I tell you what, I'll pop off to my place and grab some lunch and then I'll be back. Is that okay?"

"Fine." Nora assured.

He waved and headed off. Nora began to scratch her legs so opened the flea powder Humphrey had brought and sprinkled it by the piles of books heaped up in front of the window. She was tempted to pour it in her socks.

A woman arrived who looked like a Beryl Cook painting. She wore enormous glasses.

"Bargain Book Yard?" She simpered.

"That way." Nora indicated.

The woman tittered and followed the directions.

Nora peered out of the window to see Paperback Pam talking with Penny, who had a souvenir shop and was placing small windmills and fairies on sticks in the flowerpots outside her window. Puffs of smoke sailed from Paperback Pam.

By the time Paperback Pam had finished her cigarette, streams of bargain hunters had arrived. Nora decided to go home for lunch since all the benches about the town would be wet and the kitchen was invaded.

"Are you sure you will be alright for half an hour?" Nora asked Paperback Pam.

"Of course. I know how to work the till and I'll take down any messages."

"Remember, it's a twenty percent discount on books only marked in red pencil."

"Okay. I remember how to do discounts on the till so I shall be fine."

"I have my phone with me if there's a problem. The number is in the file under the counter."

"Go and have lunch, Nora." Paperback Pam smiled. "The shop will be well."

"Okay. Bye."

Nora left The Secondhand Bookworm, heading up the steep hill to where her flat was located at the top, above The Fudge Pantry. The Fudge Pantry window looked stuffed full of delicious offerings. Nora was having a break from sampling Oliver Braithwaite's new November fudge since she had put on an extra dress size because of his delicious fudgy delights. He waved at her, pointing at the window to try and tempt her.

Nora laughed, shook her head and unlocked the door next to the shop, deciding to plan a quick November clean if the Duke of Cole was going to be her lunch guest!

When Nora returned to The Secondhand Bookworm after her lunch, Clive was speaking with Paperback Pam.

"Ah, Nora." Paperback Pam greeted. "Do we give discounts to other booksellers?"

Nora saw the box of books Clive had pulled out, which was bursting at the seams.

"I think we can do that." She smiled. "We offer a ten percent discount for trade."

"That's awesome. Thanks!" Clive appreciated.

Paperback Pam began to run the prices of the books through the till.

Once she had deposited her bag and coat down the walkway that led to under the first staircase, Nora helped. The total came to just over two hundred pounds with Clive's discount. He paid and hoisted up the box.

"Give me a call if you every want a tour of my books. Or a coffee?" Clive said to Nora.

Nora smiled.

"Thanks. Bye, Clive."

He winked.

"Blessings." He said and headed off.

Nora looked at Paperback Pam, but she was thumbing through a paperback.

"I'll have my lunch now, Nora." She decided. "Are there any nice cafes around here?"

"The Flowery Teacup down Market Street is good." Nora replied.

"I shall go there."

"Have a nice lunch."

"Bye, Nora." Paperback Pam said and left.

Nora dropped down into the swivel chair. She wondered if there were many people in the Bargain Book Yard and hoped business would pick up. With the sun now out it usually drew visitors to Castletown so it could be a busy afternoon.

As she sat reading the Skype chat messages, a woman arrived.

"Oh I almost paid for this next door" She apologised, waving a book from the bargain trolley.

"Oh dear." Nora sympathised.

"Yes, quite. They're having renovations in there and I was screamed at when I stepped inside."

"I think it's a stressful situation for them." Nora placated.

"What a lovely shop this is. Are they all secondhand?"

"We stock a selection of new books." Nora explained, looking for the price in her bargain copy of 'Delia Smith's Happy Christmas' cookery book.

"Such as?"

"Oh. Erm…new ordnance survey maps…"

"What are they?"

"Walking maps for areas throughout Great Britain." Nora replied, pointing beneath the counter at the front.

The woman leaned back and had a rummage.

"Oh I say. Lovely and pink. Oh I see. Seatown and the South Downs, Landranger 197. Is it fifteen pounds because it's weatherproof?"

"Yes.

"It shows you how to get to the sand dunes, ah, and endless historical buildings, with walks through the hills. I'll take one."

"Thanks." Nora took it, pleased.

"What other new books?" The woman asked.

"Here are some new books showing a range of the art of Arthur Rackham. This one with Alice in Wonderland on the front is nice."

"The Arthur Rackham Treasury. Hmm, lovely."

While the lady browsed, several customers arrived seeking the Bargain Book Yard. A man asked for cricket books and a woman for crime novels. Business was starting to pick up.

By the time Paperback Pam returned over half an hour later, Nora had sold eight new books to her first customer, reordered them online, directed endless people to the Bargain Book Yard, had three telephone calls, sold three hundred pounds worth of books from the antiquarian section to five American tourists, looked for some railway books for Cara's customer in Seatown and was in dire need of a cup of tea.

"I'll make us some." Paperback Pam said once she had placed her handbag and coat safely away and brushed her thick bowl haircut.

"Thanks." Nora appreciated as more people headed towards the counter carrying bargain books.

Paperback Pam was gone for ages.

Nora kept trying to look down the walkway into the back room for her but was endlessly interrupted. After a while she began to panic. When Paperback Pam finally returned carrying tea she smiled mildly.

"I had to make a round of tea for four men." She explained. "And then I tidied up the paperbacks in the Bargain Book Yard."

Nora stared.

"We don't usually make tea for customers." She said.

"Don't we? Well they saw me making ours and asked if they could have some."

"The cheek!" Nora said.

"Oh I think they were thirsty and they are going to be buying bargain books." Paperback Pam defended.

Nora felt her lip begin to curl in a snarl.

"Mind if I take this up to the paperback room and continue? Thanks."

Paperback Pam turned to go but Nora stopped her.

"Please take a walkie-talkie." She offered.

"Alright then." Paperback Pam reluctantly accepted, turned and headed off.

Nora bristled for a full ten minutes, before taking out her iPhone and texting her mum.

'Mum. Was Paperback Pam selfish at the school?'

There was no reply so Nora decided to text her sister Heather, who entertained Nora for the next half an hour with sympathetic and amusing replies.

"Thanks for the tea. We've left our mugs in the sink." A large warty man interrupted Nora.

Nora looked up from cutting out some price labels.

"Oh. You're welcome." She replied tightly.

"We couldn't find anything we wanted."

"No, but we had a good read of some of your books." A second man said.

"You should get some sofas out there." A third man suggested.

Nora's lips pursed.

"We're not a library." She said as politely as she could.

They all looked offended.

"No worries then."

"Don't freak out."

"Calm down!"

"Let's get going." A fourth man said, tutted at Nora, and they all left.

"Grrrr." Nora glowered after them and stood up to serve some customers.

Paperback Pam emerged an hour later to collect the keys for the toilet.

"Can I use the toilet after you?" Nora asked.

"Alright." Paperback Pam said and headed off.

When she came back, Nora was busy serving a walking group that had trodden wet mud throughout the entire shop and were apologising.

"That's okay. I can run a damp mop over the floors and stairs."

"But your carpet. Is it ruined?" A man who looked like Shakespeare asked.

Nora leaned over the counter. She grimaced.

"Oh. It happens this time of the year. I'll let it dry out and then give it a hoover."

They apologised as Nora ran their books through the till, bagged them up, took their money and when they had gone, she turned to Paperback Pam and did a double take at the empty space.

Nora hunted around for her, even checking the back room, kitchen and Bargain Book Yard. She grabbed her walkie-talkie.

"Hello, Pam? Are you upstairs?"

There was a crackle and then a beep.

"Yes, Nora. I'm sorting W-Z."

Nora shook her head.

"Please may I use the toilet?"

There was a long silence and then:

"Give me ten minutes and I'll be down. I need a cigarette."

Nora stared at the walkie-talkie, beginning to jiggle and cross her legs. It was a miracle she was able to sell several piles of books to six people while she waited, and when Paperback Pam finally came down, Nora grabbed the shop keys and fled upstairs.

Paperback Pam was reading when Nora returned.

"Did you notice the mud throughout the entire shop?!" Nora was horrified.

Paperback Pam finished the sentence she was reading before looking at Nora with a smile.

"I did. It's terrible."

A man strolled into the front of the shop from the back room at that moment.

"Hey. Tell Georgina to get her finger out." He said, hostile.

Nora stared.

"Pardon?"

"I said, tell Georgina to get her finger out. This place is disgusting." He repeated, shook his head and stormed off.

Nora and Paperback Pam stared after him.

"I'll run a mop around the whole shop." Nora sighed and left before Paperback Pam could say anything.

In the kitchen, Nora rummaged around the cupboard for the mop bucket. The mop was leaning in the corner by the door frame. She filled up the bucket with hot water and a squirt of washing up liquid, listening to two people arguing over a book in the yard.

As she stood dipping the mop into the water, swirling it around and getting it wet, a man loomed up behind her.

"Game of Thrones?" He asked.

Nora turned.

The man was tall with a beard and no moustache. He was bald so looked as though his head was on upside down.

"If we had a copy it would be in the paperback room in the attic."

"No DVDs?"

"Er…no, this is a bookshop."

"Silly me. Thanks." He said, heading into the Bargain Book Yard.

Nora picked up the mop and the bucket and fled upstairs, ignoring Paperback Pam who called after her, "When can I have a cigarette break?"

It took Nora ten minutes to clean the whole shop. The paperback room carpet was filthy but there was no remedying that, so instead she spent the time carefully damp mopping each floor, salvaging the linoleum, as well as each step. When she reached the bottom floor landing, the mop water was obscene. Nora carried it through to the front of the shop and stood on the kerb, waiting for a red car to pass, before sloshing it into the road and down the drain.

"Do you have permission to do that?" A confrontational voice asked.

Nora knew it was Hugh.

"Yes." Nora smiled cheerfully.

"Who from?" Hugh demanded.

He was as filthy as the stairs had been in The Secondhand Bookworm. The illuminous yellow trousers and coat he wore were caked with and spattered in mud.

"Paul at the Chamber of Commerce said I could pour a bucket of water down this drain every day if I needed to." Nora made up.

Hugh scoffed.

"Yeah, right." He smirked slightly, eyeing Nora thoughtfully. "You're a bit of alright, you are."

Nora decided that was his way of complimenting her so let it go.

"Are you having a good day?" She asked.

"No. Three toilets were blocked in the short term car park. I think some footballers went on a pie binge last night and that was the result."

Nora almost doubled up laughing.

Hugh grinned.

"You should see the state of the roads by His Lordship's castle gates. There were horses and…well…you know."

Nora continued to laugh.

"How about your bookshop? I bet you've had no customers. What a mad trade to be in." Hugh said rudely.

Nora sobered.

"We're doing really well. Can you read?" She retorted.

Hugh's eyes widened.

"Yeah!" He defended.

"Well why don't you have a look at our books one day? But you'll have to remove your boots first." She suggested.

"I might if I want." He shrugged, suddenly distracted. "That git!"

Nora stood quickly aside as Hugh shot past her, stomping heavily towards a teenage boy who had thrown an empty crisp packet into the road. Nora picked up her bucket and retreated inside the shop, where Paperback Pam looked harassed, serving customers. Nora felt guilty.

Once she had returned the mop and bucket to the kitchen, told a man she couldn't make him a cup of tea, directed three people to the sports books on the top floor, front room, Nora told Paperback Pam to take a cigarette break.

"Thank you, Nora. I added up the takings for you. Look, I wrote it there."

Nora almost fell over.

"Nine hundred and thirty pounds!" She exclaimed.

"Yes, we're doing well, today." Paperback Pam said, pleased, grabbed her cigarette packet and lighter and left.

Nora Skyped Cara and Betty and told them the total so far. She asked how they were getting on in the Seatown shop.

'*Wow! Well done! Just gone over six hundred here! –Cara xxx*'

'*That's brilliant. I'll have to come over and check out your bargain yard. I don't know when though!*'

'*It's not as good as yours xx*'

'*We have more room here, that's why xx*'

'*Just had Mr Hill on the phone and he wants to sell his books LOL xxx*'

Nora grimaced.

Mr Hill was a regular of The Secondhand Bookworm branches. He had been buying and selling the same ten or fifteen books for decades. Georgina allowed him because she said it was his reason for existing, but it meant that Mr Hill would plague both shops with his phone calls from various booths or his smelly house, planning to bring in his books, sell them, and then make arrangements to buy them back, week after week, after week. Nora was just pleased he was focusing on Seatown that week so far.

'*I hope he doesn't annoy me xx*'

'*I'll tell him all his books are there haha*'

'*Please don't!!!*'

'*Okay. Meow xxx*'

Nora chuckled.

A loud duck quacking told Nora she had received a text message.

'*No.*' Her mum had replied in answer to Nora's question about selfishness in Paperback Pam.

Nora sighed and decided to text Humphrey.

'*How's your day going?*' She wrote and pressed send.

A moment later:

'*Hi. I miss you. Busy. Looking forward to the autumn festival tonight. Apparently there's a Ferris wheel xxx*'

Nora sat up.

'*That's brilliant. We'll have to go on it x*'

'*Wouldn't miss it. Love you xx*'

Nora stared.

"Oh dear." She sighed, bent over and began to scratch her legs.

6 THE ABSEILING DUKE

For the rest of the afternoon in The Secondhand Bookworm it seemed as though the people in the antique shop were determined to give Nora a headache. Sawing, drilling and deafening hammering vibrated against the walls for hours. At one point, the man who ran the shop came in, covered in wood shavings. He had an upturned nose like a pig's and a beard like a goat's. Nora tried to keep her mouth straight as she remembered Felix's name for him as Pig-Goat.

"I need access to your yard." Pig-Goat said.

"I'm sorry. The whole area is covered at the moment and the gate padlocked."

Pig-Goat's shoulders dropped.

"I saw that from my windows but I really need access." He whined.

"What do you need to do?"

"Drill a hole in the wall for access."

"Though an outside wall?"

"Yeah."

"I'm sorry, but this week the yard is part of the shop and there are customers out there browsing books."

"What kind of a woman puts books in her outside yard?" Pig-Goat grumbled, brushing the wood shavings from his shoulders onto the carpet. Nora assumed he was moaning about Georgina.

"It's for Black Friday." Nora defended.

"Oh. Good sales endeavour." Pig-Goat begrudgingly praised. "Is she about?"

"Who?"

"The bane of my life. The owner."

"Georgina?"

"That's her."

"No, she's not here this week."

Pig-Goat snorted, like a pig-goat, lifted his arm and waved as he turned.

"Bye." He said, wacked his hand on a ceiling beam, swore and stomped off.

Nora's lips trembled with laughter.

"Do I know you?" A man asked.

Nora turned to where he stood next to the counter, staring at her.

"Erm…I don't think so."

He shrugged and left.

"Excuse me, how do you spell Castletown?" A lady asked, entering the shop with a pen and a postcard, the latter from one of the spinners on the pavement.

Nora stared.

"Pardon?"

"I want to send this card to my son. Of Castletown. But I can't spell it."

"It says it on the front." Nora pointed.

"Oh! So it does. Thanks."

She stood at the counter writing for ages while Nora sold more books.

"May I read you this, to see what you think?" Postcard-Lady asked once Nora had finished serving a customer.

Nora wrote down the sale and nodded.

"Okay."

"Ahem. 'Chris. I don't think you should divorce Tonya.'"

Nora looked up.

"She may well have been philandering but she's the mother of your children and if you showed her the attention she is obviously craving, she wouldn't have cheated on you with your brothers. Listen to me and heed my words, Chris, or Pastor Jim will have to speak about the affair to the congregation at Sunday service and you won't like that. Having a lovely time in Castle-Town, mum xxxx"

Postcard-Lady looked up expectantly.

Nora just stared.

"Can you imagine what I've been going through? It's the scandal of our village. I can't look people in the face. He can't divorce Tonya, it will shame me. Oh, woe is me." She sighed, shaking her head. "How much for the postcard."

"Thirty pence."

"That's expensive! Oh, well. I suppose you can't put a price on valuable moral guidance. Here you go, dear."

"Do you have anything smaller?" Nora asked.

"No, just twenty pound notes." Postcard-Lady said.

Nora counted out the change and passed it to Postcard-Lady, who continued to gossip about her son until Paperback Pam came down, smelling strongly of cigarettes.

Nora stared.

She didn't dare ask if Paperback Pam had been smoking in the paperback room! But she had her suspicions.

"I'm finished for the day, Nora." Paperback Pam decided.

Nora looked at the clock.

"Oh, I thought you were here until five."

"I may have told Georgina that but I'm tired so I'll be going now."

"Mind if I go to the toilet, to see me through the last hour?" Nora asked.

"If you insist." Paperback Pam said.

Nora grabbed the keys and ran before Paperback Pam could change her mind.

After using the loo, Nora went and examined the paperback room, which was exceptionally tidy and sorted, but which was already being demolished by a large man in a tweed suit.

When she returned downstairs, Paperback Pam was being asked for a magnifying glass by a woman who was moaning that the print was too small in one of her bargain books.

"No, we don't have one." Paperback Pam assumed, rummaging under the counter while wearing her thick light grey coat and holding her handbag.

Nora decided not to reveal that they did have one in case the lady spent ages reading the book at the counter.

"Well, I'll leave this then." The lady said, slammed it down on the cash book, turned and left.

Paperback Pam followed her.

"Have a nice evening, Nora." She said.

"Thank you." Nora bade and when Paperback Pam had gone, Nora let out a long, low growl.

'I'm on my own now.' She Skyped to Seatown and added a sad face.

The pen started to move.

'Where's Paperback Pam?'

'Decided to go home.'

'Can she do that?'

'Well, she did it anyway…'

'Annoying.'

'Yes. But I finally solved the mystery of Bellerophon Books!'

'Really?!!! How???'

'The owner showed up and introduced himself. He has a lair down Market Street and wants me to send him victims.'

'LOL. Have you taken more money? We're on eight hundred and fifty three pounds! Meow!'

Nora smiled, turned and added up the takings. Her eyes popped.

'One thousand five hundred and ten pounds here!'

'O M Gosh!!!' Cara Skyped back and then added a row of happy faces.

Nora spent the rest of the afternoon selling another whopping seven hundred pounds worth of books. The Bargain Book Yard was a mammoth success and despite hyperventilating as she threw everyone out so as to close up, Nora was pleased to have reached over two thousand three hundred pounds, which was a rare sum for The Secondhand Bookworm, even in summer.

Once all the stragglers, dawdlers, foot-draggers and slowpokes had been ousted out of every corner of the shop and Nora had dragged in everything from outside, she closed the door, turned the sign to 'CLOSED' and began to cash up.

"Excuse me."

Nora almost screamed as a man emerged from the darkened depths of the shop and appeared by the computer.

"Oh my goodness me!" She exclaimed, dropping two bags of coins she had been counting out. "I thought everyone had gone."

"Oh, I'm terribly sorry. I was using your outside loo. You must have overlooked me." The man replied.

"What?" Nora asked, flatly.

The man held up a book.

"If I put this by until Friday, will I get fifty percent off?" He asked

Nora was still distracted and confounded that he had used the outside loo.

"Did you say you used our outside loo?"

"Yes." He smiled mildly. "The book?"

Nora gave an exasperated laugh and started to pick up the coin bags.

"Yes, yes. Why not?" She asked, a little hysterically.

"Thank you. I washed my hands in your kitchen sink. I hope you don't mind." He said, heading for the door.

"Of course not!" Nora laughed and followed him so as to unlock.

He passed her the book.

"My name is Kenny."

"Thanks Kenny!" Nora said joyfully, unlocking the door.

He smiled and headed off.

Nora shut the door and felt like bursting into tears.

Once Nora had cashed up, she returned to the Bargain Book Yard, wondering what Kenny would have done had she locked up both doors and headed off home for the night. She checked to make sure that no one else was lurking about and switched off the pumpkin face lights, her thoughts lingering on the Duke of Cole. Nora realised that she was nervous about seeing him abseiling down one of his castle turrets.

Before she set the alarm to leave, Nora googled the Duke's castle on her iPhone and read that the tallest turret the Duke of Cole had had built stood at thirty nine meters high. It was called the Godwin Tower and had been renovated in the Duke's rebuilding endeavour to restore it to its original height and grandeur. Nora blanched.

The Duke had always bought mountaineering books and had a vast collection of that subject of books in his private library, so Nora knew he was a good climber, but she didn't like the idea of seeing him abseiling down a thirty nine meter stone tower and was surprised at how worried she was.

"Get a grip, Nora." She told herself firmly, setting the alarm. "Poker face."

Nora decided she would have to hide her concern from everyone and trust in the Duke's proficiency. But she might close her eyes.

The Autumn Supper and Festival at the castle opened at six o'clock. The castle and grounds were closed to the public from October 31st through to the first Monday of April every year, so nobody had been able to see the preparations being made for the festival. Everyone was excited.

Entrance was free and parts of the castle would be open for autumn produce shows, with large parts of the grounds hosting stalls, shows and rides. There was even a famous tiny donkey coming called 'Tiny Tim', which was causing a wave of anticipation. Cara had told Nora that dogs were allowed and there would be a dog show.

Nora had arranged to meet Humphrey, Cara, Seymour, Felix, Heather and Milton at her flat and they would walk down to the main castle gates together to meet Georgina, Troy, Betty, Roger, Cal and others. Paperback Pam had been invited but had declined.

Once she was home, Nora had a shower and changed, arranged her hair with autumn flowers and fruits in a headband, fed her pet bearded dragon Beardie his crickets, and ran down the stairs when the first of her callers knocked her front door.

"Evening." Humphrey greeted smoothly.

He was leaning against her doorframe, looking handsome in his wax jacket, jeans, boots and baseball cap.

Humphrey went to kiss her but Nora wrapped her arms around him instead for a hug.

"Are you okay?" Humphrey asked against her hair.

"Yes, fine!" Nora assured, though she was pleased to see Cara and Seymour approaching, holding hands. Cara was walking Arthur.

"Arthur!"

Humphrey stepped back as Nora greeted the bulldog. He crouched down too and fussed over him.

"Bah. I'm beginning to regret getting this dog." Seymour joked, jealously.

"Hi Seymour." Nora greeted her brother and gave him a hug.

"Your book." Cara said meaningfully, handing her the third 'Jeeves and Wooster' first edition for the Duke.

"Thanks." Nora smiled.

They climbed the stairs and Nora served a round of apple juice as they waited, the men listening to Nora and Cara recount their experiences with customers.

"One lady screamed when I refused to give her fifty percent off." Cara said, using Nora's hair brush to groom Arthur.

Nora giggled.

"Betty almost had a fight with a man, too. He called her an old hag when she refused to discount his train book from the shop shelves, so she threw it violently in the bin."

Everyone laughed.

"I'm glad it's not just me dealing with maddos all day." Nora said, pleased.

When her brother Milton and their sister Heather arrived with Felix, they set off, Felix disappointed at having missed out on the apple juice.

"There will be plenty to eat and drink at the festival." Nora assured, giving him a hug.

Crowds of people were arriving at the castle and parking seemed to be bedlam. Hugh walked past and told them that the council were opening up several fields at the front of the town for cars to park.

"You should see it." He laughed mockingly. "It's a joke."

Nora shook her head and they reached the entrance.

"Nora!" Georgina's voice called.

The group spotted Georgina standing with Troy, Mrs Pickering, who was Georgina's mother, Mrs Pickering's almost-deaf brother Orville, Cal, who worked part-time in Seatown, Betty, and Roger, gathered by a toffee apple cart. Roger was reading a paper.

"Hello!" Nora greeted.

"I heard! Cara told me how much you took today! Well done. Expect a significant bonus at the end of the week, Nora!" Georgina praised happily and gave Nora a hug.

"Well done." Troy agreed, biting into his toffee apple with a crunch.

"Thanks. It has been very busy."

"Do you need any more hands?" Georgina asked. "Cara told me that Pam went home early. Was she okay?"

"Yes, she was fine. And…the paperback room looks lovely." Nora replied.

"She didn't just do the paperbacks did she?"

"That's why we call her Paperback Pam." Cara piped in.

"Oh dear." Georgina sighed.

They walked towards the castle gates. Nora felt Humphrey take hold of her hand.

"It's usually quieter in the morning." Nora mused, considering the suggestion of extra help. "But it can get manic in the afternoon."

"Felix. Are you free any weekdays this week?"

"Eh?" Felix looked up from his iPod and pulled out an ear bud.

"Are you at college all week?"

"Oh, yes, sorry. Blast. Sad emoticon." Felix replied.

"Hmm. Troy and I are in London for the morning tomorrow and then cooking for the Thanksgiving dinner, but I can always send mum over if you need her. Just give me a call."

Mrs Pickering smiled willingly.

"I'm with Nora tomorrow." Roger pointed out flatly. "It's not like I'm disabled."

Nora and Georgina looked at one another and hid their giggles.

The Secondhand Bookworm party passed through the opened castle gates and walked along the lantern lined path to where the trees parted to reveal the grand front façade and large historical jousting grounds. They all stopped dead.

"Wow!" Cal exclaimed.

"Amazing!" Cara breathed.

"Incredible!" Georgina gasped.

"This is awesome!" Troy grinned.

"Awesome sauce!" Seymour added, impressed.

"Groovy! Like a drive in movie." Milton admired.

The festival was magnificent. The whole front grounds had been transformed, with stalls twinkling with lights, the large Ferris Wheel to the left, an open arena in the centre, craft displays, a band on a stage, amazing decorations, the scents of sizzling foods and mulled wine and fruits drifting in the night air. Tiny Tim, the little donkey, was being admired and fussed over in a special paddock. There were opportunities to have your photograph taken standing next to him.

The front of the castle had been illuminated with blue and orange lights. Nora's stomach clenched when she saw the Godwin Tower. There was movement at the top.

"Oh yes. His Grace shall be abseiling down the turret to open the festival." Cara said, noticing Nora staring.

"Like Gustav Graves in the 'Die Another Day' James Bond movie?" Seymour grinned.

"What?" Cara laughed.

"That was a parachute entrance." Cal pointed out.

"Abseiling down a turret is more impressive." Heather said.

"It's a tower." Nora said, looking away.

Cara smirked, knowingly.

"Oh Nora, how pretty your hair is." Betty admired as they headed into the festival.

"Thanks." Nora grinned.

"Very pretty." Humphrey muttered in Nora's ear and kissed her cheek.

Nora smiled at him, fondly.

"Are we okay?" He asked, drawing her slightly aside.

"Why do you keep asking me that?" Nora chuckled, not meeting his eyes.

"Well, a few weeks ago you said we should break up and I convinced you we should stay together. Are you okay with that? Really?"

Nora cleared her throat.

"I love hanging out with you, Humphrey. I told you my feelings for you were as a friend."

Humphrey drew her close and wrapped his arms around her.

"I love you." He whispered.

Nora closed her eyes.

"Come on, love birds." Milton called.

Nora drew away from Humphrey, who took her hand and remained close to her. She glanced at Cara and Betty who gave her a look.

"Oh Cara, you have to enter Arthur into the dog show!" Georgina exclaimed.

While Georgina, Cara and Mrs Pickering organised that, everyone else spread out to explore the festival grounds. The Giant Pumpkin competition was incredible.

"That one could be Cinderella's coach." Heather pointed out.

There would be scarecrow making, spinning wheel demonstrations, food tasting, cider tasting, apple pressing, apple bobbing, face painting, fireworks, dancing and more. A large stall advertised the Duke's favourite charity to which the monies raised from the festival would go. It was called Aid to the Church in Need, which the Duke, a practicing Catholic, supported not only through funds and events but through volunteer work abroad.

Before anything could get started, the free programmes explained that there would be an opening greeting from the Mayor, who arrived and mounted the band stage.

"Good evening everyone, and welcome to Castletown's Autumn Supper and Festival hosted by our illustrious Duke of Cole," the Mayor announced, "who is preparing to open the evening by abseiling down Godwin Tower!"

There were deafening cheers, shouts and clapping. The Duke of Cole appeared to be very popular. A spotlight swung up to the top of the tower. Nora held her breath as a figure held up his arms and then walked to the edge of the turret.

"Oh my." Betty fanned her programme before her face.

"Awesome." Seymour grinned.

Cameras flashed and people continued to cheer.

Nora could hardly bare to watch as the Duke climbed over the edge. There was rope prepared that ran down the whole length of the tower to the bottom, and the Duke had a support staff with him at the top as well as awaiting him at the bottom, but it was clear to see he was confident in what he was doing.

A drum began to play and everyone clapped in time to its steady beat. Nora was filled with dizzy admiration. She watched as the Duke eased easily from the wall and began down the tower, sleek, smooth and professional.

"Our Duke of Cole, or as we fondly call him, Duke of Castletown." The Mayor said into the microphone as the Duke smoothly reached the ground.

Everyone cheered and Nora found herself clapping madly and being hugged by Heather and Cara.

"Not bad." Humphrey had to admit.

He grinned at Nora knowingly.

"Now as the Duke prepares to join us, where he will be judging tonight's dog show and various competitions, I would like to invite everyone to enjoy the festivities. Supper in the castle will begin at seven thirty. Everyone is welcome. Good evening and happy festival!"

Everyone cheered again, the music stared and people began to explore.

"Bookworm alert!" Cal told Nora.

They both noticed Spencer who was with his wife and occult friend, Mal. Quickly, Cal and Nora dived behind the apple cider tent.

Arthur was registered for the dog show which would take place at seven. Meanwhile, the bookshop group made their way around the festival, admiring the stalls, aware that the Duke of Cole had arrived and was mingling with the crowds.

Nora noticed the Duke as she was browsing through a selection of autumn jams and chutneys on a stall covered in lights. She became aware that he was watching her and her heart gave a small leap when she saw him shaking hands with several men, gaze levelled upon her.

"Here comes the Duke!" Cara whispered hard, nudging Nora's arm repetitively so she almost dropped a jar of sloe jam.

Nora smiled to see him make a beeline for their group.

"Good evening." The Duke of Cole smiled, shaking hands with Georgina, followed by Mrs Pickering and Troy, who fawned over him breathlessly.

When he reached Nora he paused to shake Humphrey's hand first and then took hold of Nora's.

"Miss Jolly." The Duke said, staring pointedly into Nora's eyes.

"Good evening, Your Grace." Nora smiled with a small curtsey. "Congratulations on a magnificent...erm...descent."

The Duke grinned and his shoulders shook with gentle laughter.

"Thank you. I wonder if you would you care to join me in my library this evening. Please, bring your friends and colleagues. I have a book I would like you to see."

The Duke's steady blue gaze encompassed the bookworm party who looked amazed and delighted.

"It would be our honour, Your Grace." Nora replied, aware that he was still holding her hand.

Humphrey was staring at their joined hands pointedly. The Duke seemed to remember and let go. He gave a small bow.

"I shall be opening the supper and having a bite to eat. Perhaps you would permit my valet Jeeves to show you the way at eight where it would be my pleasure to join you?"

"Thank you." Nora nodded.

The Duke's attention lingered on Nora for a long moment until he was reluctantly led away by his entourage to meet a group of waiting people.

Everyone gathered around Nora, excitedly.

"Please date him, Nora!" Cara whispered hard.

"Hey." Humphrey looked annoyed.

"He seems besotted with you, Nora." Georgina chuckled, throwing Humphrey an apologetic look.

"I wonder what book he's pleased about." Roger mused.

"Oh, this is very exciting." Mrs Pickering chipped in, rubbing her gloved hands together.

Everyone agreed that is was and spent the next hour mentioning it as they enjoyed the festival.

While Cara walked Arthur around the centre arena before the gathering of judges, which included the Duke, Humphrey and Nora leaned over the wooden fences, chatting and watching.

"I get it." Humphrey sighed, throwing a handful of malted pumpkin spice popcorn into his mouth and chewing morosely. "He's a Duke. Who wouldn't be attracted to him?"

Nora nudged his arm.

"Let's just enjoy the festival." Nora smiled.

He shrugged, looking moody, throwing glances towards the Duke who seemed busy ticking boxes as he watched Arthur.

Nora smiled as she watched too.

Two bookworms had also entered dogs into the competition. Nora was amused to see Crossword-Lady leading her daughter's Yorkshire terrier, and a lady who collected books on lace-making with a Chihuahua.

"Try these!" Heather told Nora, thrusting a bag of cinnamon apple chips under her nose.

Nora took some eagerly.

The bookworms watched in anticipation as the results of the dog show were announced. There were awards for the following:

1) The most obedient dog
2) The dog that looked most like its owner (Cara looked aghast)
3) The best bitch
4) The best male
5) The waggiest tail
6) The shiniest nose
7) The cutest bark
8) The dog that the Duke would most like to take home

Nora laughed, clapped and cheered with everyone as the awards were given. Arthur won the most obedient dog award and everyone took photos as the Duke pinned a blue rosette on Arthur's collar. Cara was delighted and everyone fussed over Arthur who looked bored.

Next the Duke chose the best giant pumpkin and handed out rosettes and shook hands. Nora watched the way he was with people, both admiring him and feeling sorry for him since she understood he was a private person who liked his solitude.

Supper at the castle promised to be exciting. People were making their way along the wide, winding paths to the grand castle entrance which had been decorated with lights and impressive autumn garlands. Dogs were permitted and the buffets were spread out in three grand rooms. The bookshop party joined the affair and were soon enjoying plates of bacon and squash gratin, pumpkin pies, purple sweet potato pottage, and delicious desserts.

The Duke mingled politely, occasionally meeting Nora's eyes.

At almost eight o'clock, Jeeves appeared at Nora's side.

"My lady?" He smiled, knowingly.

The Secondhand Bookworm group eagerly left the supper halls and were led through the castle into the Duke's private quarters. When they entered the library, Georgina and Mrs Pickering thought they were in Heaven. They began to explore the vast room, with its galleries of books, filigree cases, magnificent seating area and endless special tomes.

Jeeves and two footmen had just served a round of hot mulled wine when the Duke of Cole arrived, accompanied by Marlowe, his miniature schnauzer. Everyone stood and Marlowe skipped over to greet Nora before befriending a curious Arthur.

"Your Grace." Nora greeted as he walked towards her.

The Duke smiled around at the gathering and accepted a glass of hot wine from Jeeves.

"Thank you all for coming."

"It's our pleasure, Your Grace!"

"Thank you for the invitation!"

"What a magnificent library you have!"

Everyone spoke excitedly at once. The Duke grinned, standing next to Nora.

"As you know I have properties throughout England and moved to Castletown from my estates in Butteryhaugh, Northumberland and James Hall in Norfolk." He told them.

Everyone nodded eagerly. Nora was impressed he had a stately house named after himself.

"Occasionally I visit James Hall and have been looking through the large amount of books, papers and documents that are part of the estates."

"How wonderful, Your Grace." Georgina said, dreamily.

The Duke smiled. He then placed his glass on a small, carved oak table and walked over to another whereupon he picked up a medium sized leather bound tome.

"Last week I discovered this and thought you would find it interesting."

He was looking at Nora specifically, but everyone edged closer.

Nora took the book from the Duke.

"If you open it at the page I've marked you will see an interesting chapter." The Duke told Nora gently.

She smiled at him and opened the tome. Cara placed her chin on Nora's shoulder, eagerly.

"Oh. It's handwritten." Nora realised.

Beautiful penmanship decorated the pages. The chapter heading read, 'The Ghosts of Castletown Fortress'. Nora looked up and met the Duke's eyes. He nodded, knowing she would find it fascinating.

"One of my ancestors came to our property here, two centuries ago, and documented the ghosts of the estate." The Duke told everyone as Nora stared at the pages. "Her name was Lady Jessica and she was our family's ghost hunter."

There were murmurs of interest and excited whispers. Georgina examined the book with Nora while the Duke picked up his glass and moved to the enormous fireplace. He gave the logs a poke so the flames rose higher with a delicious crackle. He then leaned against the marble mantelpiece looking every bit like a Duke.

"Perhaps you would like to read it aloud Miss Jolly?" The Duke of Cole invited.

Nora looked at him.

"Oh yes, do Nora. You have such a lovely voice." Betty encouraged.

"Go on Nora." Cara agreed.

Georgina nodded and everyone settled down in the armchairs and sofas around the fire, with Arthur and Marlowe sitting at their feet, all staring at her expectantly. Humphrey smiled and the Duke watched her steadily, while Roger nodded for Jeeves to top up his wine glass and seemed to be enjoying himself immensely.

"Very well." Nora nodded and cleared her throat.

She began, aware of the Duke watching her intensely.

"November the twenty first, the year of Our Lord Eighteen Hundred and three." She read.

Everyone 'oooed' since it was the exact same day and month as *that* day.

"Did you know that?" Nora asked the Duke.

"Yes." He smiled.

"Spooky." Cal grinned.

Nora continued.

"I have been staying in Castletown for three weeks now, having interviewed several people in the small town, the local villages and of course our staff on the estate. I have discovered four ghosts specific to the fortress here. The first ghost of note is the apparition of Earl Godwin, who was thrown from the tallest tower."

Everyone looked at the Duke.

"Hmm." He nodded. "It is said he was betrayed by his household who let Elizabethan priest hunters into the fortress. He was hounded up to the tower and thrown off by the notorious Richard Topcliffe for hiding hunted Catholic priests."

Everyone stared.

"Have you ever seen him, Your Grace?" Nora asked in the silence.

The Duke shook his head.

"No, but Jeeves has."

Everyone looked at Jeeves. He gave a small bow.

"I have indeed, Your Grace. Falling gracefully past the window and making the sign of the cross as he descended."

"That's what people have purported to see." The Duke added with a small smile.

Everyone looked intrigued.

"Was your abseiling tonight in memory of the Earl, Your Grace?" Nora asked.

The Duke stared at her.

"As a matter of fact, yes." He admitted, impressed with Nora's deduction.

She smiled knowingly, having read that the rebuilding and reconstruction of Godwin Tower had been a special project of the Duke's.

Everyone murmured their approval.

Nora skipped over the detailed account of the ghostly murdered Earl Godwin.

"The second ghost is that of a Cavalier. He is known as the Red Man. People have seen him ride his horse throughout the grounds, with his long flowing hair in ringlets, his brightly coloured clothing with trimmings and lace collar and cuffs, and a grand plumed hat. He ends his ride falling from his horse having been shot by a Roundhead who had pursued him here." Nora read.

"Oh my. That is very spooky." Betty said.

"The ghost of a small white owl is often seen in the windows of the keep and the gatehouse." Nora continued. "It is thought to be a sign of romance or good fortune."

"I say." Heather whispered with a smirk.

"The last ghost is that of a woman. She was spurned in love by the sixth Duke of Castletown. People have seen her walk through the old library for she threw herself from the keep, clutching her favourite book."

Everyone looked around the room, suddenly expecting to see her. Cara shuddered. The Duke smiled.

Nora flicked through the pages, absorbed in her own thoughts.

"Is that is?" Troy asked, making Mrs Pickering jump.

"Eh?" Uncle Orville asked, cupping a hand over his ear.

"Oh. Well, it goes into a lot of detail so I shall stop there." Nora decided.

The Duke nodded, watching her walk over to him and hand him back the book while everyone began to discuss the hauntings.

"Thank you." The Duke smiled.

"You're welcome." Nora smiled back.

They spoke briefly, watched by Humphrey, until the Duke offered to give the bookshop party a brief tour of the library before they would return to the festival. Everyone hung on the Duke's words as he showed them his special collections, allowed them to hold or look through specific tomes, and answered everyone's questions. Finally, they left the library and returned to the supper halls, where the Duke bade them all a good evening and was led by Jeeves to a group of people wishing to speak with him.

"Well, I think I'm up for some scarecrow making now." Milton announced.

"I'll join you." Cal grinned.

Felix also liked the idea so when the bookshop party was back at the autumn festival grounds, they separated and spread out to enjoy the evening.

Humphrey and Nora, Georgina and Troy, Cara and Seymour rode the Ferris wheel, admiring the Duke's castle from the top, while Betty and Roger, Mrs Pickering and uncle Orville sat in the cider tent with Arthur.

The evening ended with a magnificent firework display with the castle as the backdrop, and Nora was sure she saw the ghost of a little owl fluttering among the windows. She told Humphrey that as they walked back to his car and he said he suspected it was a sign especially for her.

She grinned and they stopped to eat some toffee apples while they waited for everyone else, bade goodbye and then all departed to set off home after an enjoyable and eventful Autumn Supper Festival.

7 ROBERT LOUIS STEVENSON IS DEAD!

Thursday morning was declared to be a 'headache day' as Hugh walked up and down the streets of Castletown with a very loud leaf blower. He spent ten minutes outside the door of The Secondhand Bookworm, fiercely blowing a pile of orange and red leaves into a pile until Nora jumped up the step and tapped his shoulder.

"Really?" She asked, glaring.

"This is the price to pay for clean streets!" Hugh defended and aimed the blower at her.

Nora continued glaring until he shrugged and set off slowly, only to return ten minutes later to start to blow his pile of leaves carefully around the corner.

After a sunny start to the day, it started to rain.

"Hopefully that'll put an end to the leaf blower." Roger said grimly as he sat reading his morning paper behind the counter.

Nora decided to add to the noise by hoovering the shop, much to Roger's annoyance.

"Honestly, woman!" He grumbled when she accidently sucked his shoelaces up Henry's nozzle.

The shop look much cleaner and as Nora was returning the hoover to the kitchen, people started to arrive at the Bargain Book Yard.

"Oh, what a lovely room!" A small lady exclaimed, hurrying past Nora in the kitchen so as to begin grabbing bargains.

"Thanks." Nora smiled.

"And it sounds so lovely with the rain pitter-pattering on the roof. Oh. Is that a pigeon?"

Nora stepped into the yard and stared. Somehow a pigeon had managed to find its way inside. It was sitting looking pleased with itself on one of the tables.

"Erm…"

It didn't even flinch when Nora drove near.

The woman laughed.

"I'm sure it will find somewhere to hide if lots of people arrive." She said and went to browse the knitting books.

Nora remained staring at the pigeon for some time before returning to the front of the shop where Roger was serving a group of customers.

"Yes. I go to the Buddhist temple every week in Newhaven." Roger was telling a plump, bald man, who looked like Buddha.

"Glad to hear it." Buddha nodded.

"Roger. There's a pigeon in the Bargain Book Yard." Nora informed him.

"Shall I put the oven on?" He teased flatly.

Nora gasped.

"I could put some food out for it."

Roger gave her a look.

"Do you have any books by Robert Louis Stevenson?" A little old lady asked.

"Robert Louis Stevenson is dead!" The man with her exclaimed.

Nora's lips twitched.

"I'm interested in all his works. I especially like his verses. For instance, the epitaph on his grave reads thus." The little old lady took a loud, deep breath.

"Under the wide and starry sky,
Dig the grave and let me lie.
Glad did I live and gladly die,
And I laid me down with a will.
This be the verse you grave for me:
Here he lies where he longed to be;
Home is the sailor, home from sea,
And the hunter home from the hill.' Isn't that marvellous!" She recited.

Nora was mesmerised.

"Yes. Well, we do get collections of his works in at times. Perhaps we have a set of his novels back here." She said, turning around to rummage on the shelves behind her.

When she turned back having searched in vain, the little old lady was halfway out the door with her husband. Nora stared. Roger smirked and went back to reading his paper.

"Some people are very strange." Nora concluded, and decided to text Humphrey about the pigeon.

She paused as she pondered his name on her list of contacts, wondering if she was encouraging him too much. He seemed to refuse to think of their relationship as no more than best friends, despite the talk they had had after the Autumn Supper and Festival while waiting by the toffee apple cart. When they had parted at his truck he had kissed her goodbye, leaving Nora exasperated. In the end she decided to text Georgina so as to leave it all in her hands.

'A pigeon has taken up residence in the Bargain
Book Yard! Hope you're having a good day! Looking
forward to tonight xx' Nora wrote and pressed send.

"Hello. Do you have anything by Voltaire? It was his birthday yesterday?" A man with a black and white striped beanie hat asked.

Roger looked up from his paper.

"I'm sure that we do."

"I am particularly interested in his satirical novella Candide, and the tragic play Zaïre." The man explained.

"Come with me." Roger gestured and took the customer away.

A knot of bargain hunters arrived.

"All of your books have thirty percent off today?" A man asked as the group moved towards the counter as if joined together.

"No. Only the books in the Bargain Book Yard, out the back." Nora indicated.

The group bent their heads together and whispered hard, before heading off for the yard.

Nora checked her watch, counting down the hours until lunchtime when she was meeting the Duke of Cole.

A text message arrived so Nora read it.

'Oh flipping heck! I'll send Humphrey over with a net. Troy and I are shopping in Harrods for the dinner tonight. Some last minute garnishes xx' Georgina had written.

Nora sighed, wondering if she should be firm with Humphrey and tell him they shouldn't see each other anymore, even though she was very fond of him as a friend.

"On this day, Blackbeard the Pirate was killed!" A loud, booming voice hollered into the shop from the doorway.

Nora almost dropped her iPhone. She stared at a large figure dressed as a swashbuckler. He stepped inside.

"On November the twenty second in the year seventeen hundred and eighteen, Blackbeard and his forces were defeated in a BLOODY WAR at the battle of Ocracoke Island!" The man said dramatically. "Blackbeard was so called because of his long black beard which he used to set on fire to terrorize his enemies! Come along to Nineveh House for all things Blackbeard and all things Pirate. This Saturday, the twenty fourth of November."

The pirate offered her a small pile of flyers.

"Oh. Thanks." Nora said, taking them.

"Hope to see you there mi heartie!" The pirate said, turned around and left.

Nora shook her head, placing the flyers on the edge of the counter by some local guides written by David Bone.

"Good morning. Do you have any sheet music by Scott Joplin?" A woman with very fluffy black hair asked. "Oh, what a lovely shop!"

"Thanks. We have a music section upstairs."

"Oh how lovely. I'll go and have a look." She smiled and set off.

Nora decided to hunt out some Robert Louis Stevenson books, inspired by the rude little old lady, so she spent a while rummaging through the shelves around the counter and along the walkway into the back room. She uncovered some small sets and displayed them on the counter, adding a few to the window.

A man arrived and leaned very close to her so as to read the books she was arranging.

Nora stared at him.

"Robert Louis Stevenson is dead, you know!" The man informed Nora.

"Erm...yes, I did."

"Dead!" He repeated, meaningfully, before setting off for the Bargain Book Yard and leaving Nora flabbergasted.

When Roger returned with his Voltaire customer, Nora slipped upstairs and gathered new copies of Robert

Louis Stevenson's novels from the new Wordsworth books section, as well as other used paperback editions from the attic room. She then displayed them in the window and a man came in and purchased one.

Nora reordered a copy of 'Treasure Island' with a smile.

"Perhaps the spirit of Blackbeard is looking down on us." She told Roger.

"You've gone potty." Roger retorted.

A text message arrived so Nora dug out her phone under the disapproving look of Roger.

'Humphrey can't get there until lunchtime. What is the pigeon doing now?' Georgina asked.

Nora decided to go and visit it.

In the Bargain Book Yard, the first lady from earlier stood gathering a large pile of knitting books while the knot of bargain hunters were gathered together by the outside loo.

"Oh, hello. These are such a bargain." The first lady said.

"Yes, they're good." Nora agreed.

The pigeon had flown onto the top of one of the cases and was preening itself.

'Preening itself.' She texted Georgina.

A moment later:

'Please make sure it doesn't poop on anyone!' Georgina asked.

"How am I supposed to do that?" Nora sighed.

She headed back to Roger and stopped dead.

"Hello, Gina."

Crossword-Lady was at the desk, speaking with Roger. They were both comparing their newspapers.

"Hello." Nora replied.

"I had come in to ask you today's literary answer in my crossword, but your nice colleague had filled it in in his own paper so he has assisted me today."

"That's good." Nora said politely. "Roger. Georgina needs me on pigeon poop duty in the Bargain Book Yard. I'll be out there if you need me."

Roger just stared.

"Perhaps it's a new film role research." Nora heard Crossword-Lady say as she headed back.

The rain was falling pleasantly on the plastic roof in the Bargain Book Yard. Nora decided to tidy up the tables while keeping an eye on the pigeon. She was sure she could hear Hugh's leaf blowing in the distance.

A new text message arrived. Nora saw that it was from Cara and included a photograph of 'Tiny Tim' the donkey from the festival the previous evening.

'He's going to be in Castletown town square on Saturday!!! Xxx' Cara wrote.

Nora chuckled.

'I can't wait!! Xxx' She sent back.

"Hello."

Nora turned and stared. One of Georgina's specialist customers, who usually only spoke to, or dealt with, Georgina, stood in the kitchen doorway.

"Oh. Hello, Percival." Nora replied.

"Georgina told me about her Bargain Book Yard. I thought I'd come and see it for myself." He said, peering curiously around.

"Yes, it's very nice." Nora smiled, glancing nervously at the pigeon and hoping it wouldn't poop on Percival.

Percival was a self-made millionaire who collected very expensive and rare books and any type of books about trains. He had the largest Hornby train collection in the world so that whenever Hornby wished to bring out a new book about their model trains, they would go to Percival's house and take photographs of his collection. Over the summer, Nora had seen Percival in his red speedos, so wasn't as intimidated by him as she had been.

Other people began to arrive, clamouring to grab bargain books, so Percival stood aside and stood contemplating the room for a few minutes, before turning and leaving without saying goodbye.

The pigeon retreated to the back of the bookcase so Nora decided it wasn't going to defecate on customers and went back to the front of the shop.

"Would you like a cup of hot chocolate?" Roger asked.

"Oh! Yes that would be wonderful."

"I'll get us one each from the delicatessen. And some spiced pumpkin biscuits." He offered, folding his paper. "My treat as a thank you for a nice evening with your royal admirer."

Nora gave him a look.

"Thanks." She accepted, pleased.

"You're welcome, Your Majesty." He teased.

More people arrived, rushing to the Bargain Book Yard with arms outstretched. They were all wearing bobble hats. Soon, The Secondhand Bookworm was swarming with people. The till was churning and beeping, books were being bagged up, and when Roger returned with hot chocolate and biscuits, he started to get stressed that the drinks would go cold because of the constant stream of buyers.

There was an eventual five minute lull so they savoured the hot chocolate, nibbled their biscuits and then went back to trading as people demanded more money off, or discounts on ordinary shop stock, or asked how much they could have off for cash!

"Excuse me, but Robert Louis Stevenson is dead." A man said, sticking his head in the doorway.

Nora was waiting for Roger to come back from the loo before she headed home for lunch with the Duke and was adding up the takings so far in the cash book. She looked up and stared.

"Erm…"

"Just so you know!" He gestured to the books in the window before stomping off.

Nora looked confused a moment. She decided to google why there was a phenomenon of people declaring that Robert Louis Stevenson was dead, but all that came up in the search results was that the author had died at aged forty four of intracerebral haemorrhage. Apparently he had been straining to open a bottle of wine on the third of December 1894 when he suddenly exclaimed to his wife, "What's that? Does my face look strange?", and collapsed and died within a few hours.

Nora cringed and finished adding up the sales. They had taken twelve hundred pounds so far and it was still very busy.

Nora placed the first edition copy of 'Very good, Jeeves' into her bag and waited impatiently for Roger. He soon came dawdling down.

"Go on then, impatient one." He said as she shrugged into her coat. "Have a date do we?"

Nora blushed.

"No." She assured.

Roger looked at her suspiciously.

"Do you need anything before I go?" She asked innocently.

"Some champagne and caviar."

Nora laughed, waved goodbye and set off from The Secondhand Bookworm as more bargain hunters arrived.

The deep autumn sunshine streamed in through the front windows of Nora's flat, making the room look inviting, warm and pretty. She had set the little dining table with a lace cloth, nice plates, glasses and her tea set, done some last minute tidying, placed autumn garlands and fruits about the room, and jumped when her doorbell rang.

Pausing to straighten her blouse and attempt to flatten down a few wisps of hair, Nora then walked down the stairs, took a breath, and opened her door to the Duke of Cole.

He stood on her front doorstep, holding a large covered dish and smiling. Jeeves was with him, holding an umbrella above the Duke. He winked at Nora.

"Good afternoon, Nora." The Duke greeted warmly.

"Good afternoon, Your Grace." Nora replied. "Please come in."

"Thank you." The Duke said, nodded to Jeeves and stepped into Nora's little entrance hall.

Jeeves turned and headed off back up the hill to the private castle entrance. Nora closed the door and found herself facing the Duke.

"How are you?" He grinned.

"Very well, thank you. You?" Nora grinned back.

"Very well." He assured.

He wiped his feet and bent down to untie the laces of his boots.

"This way." Nora said with a smile, once he had removed his footwear, turned and began up the stairs. She couldn't help but glance back as she heard him following her, her head spinning with amazement that she was having lunch alone with the Duke of Cole.

"This is lovely." The Duke admired, looking around Nora's lounge.

"Thank you. I'll put the kettle on for tea." Nora said and headed for her kitchen.

The Duke placed his covered dish on the table and followed her.

"How are things at The Secondhand Bookworm?" He asked, leaning against the edge of the worktop.

"We're currently passing through a build up to Black Friday with a discounted Bargain Book Yard. You can imagine the fun we're having with the excess of bargain book hunters."

The Duke chuckled.

"The general public is a fascinating thing."

"Isn't it?" Nora smirked, putting her kettle on a hob to boil.

"And how many members for the book club do you now have?"

Nora headed for the table and chairs and the Duke followed her.

"There are six of us so far."

The Duke nodded.

"I'm very much looking forward to it."

"I'm glad. I think you'll enjoy the books."

"And will Humphrey be joining us?" He asked lightly.

Nora cleared her throat.

"No." She replied.

They beheld one another steadily. Nora glanced away, reddening.

"What did you bring for lunch?" She asked, curiously.

With a smile, the Duke removed the lid of his dish. Nora's eyes widened as she beheld a sumptuous spread; two golden pies on a bed of salad with roasted munchkin pumpkins, seasonal garnishes and another covered dish that revealed two pumpkin muffins.

"Wow." Nora stared.

"Compliments of my chef. He's Scottish."

"Haggis pies?"

The Duke laughed.

"No."

"This is for you, Your Grace." Nora said, picking up his book.

"James." The Duke insisted.

"I don't know if I can get used to that." Nora confessed.

"No formalities between friends, Nora. Remember?"

"Of course." She nodded, glancing away to hide her chuffed grin.

"Ah. 'Very good, Jeeves'." James took the paper covering off the book with interest. "Have you read it?"

"I have."

"What happens?"

"I wouldn't want to spoil the plot for you."

"I don't mind. I'd like to hear you tell me about it over lunch? And then maybe you can tell me about the books we will be starting to read for the book club too. And your long story about Humphrey Pickering."

"Okay." Nora squeaked as the kettle started to whistle.

James watched Nora reluctantly turn away to make a pot of tea, leaving him smiling after her and starting to serve up lunch.

8 THE THANKSGIVING DINNER

That afternoon, Nora was sitting scratching her legs, convinced she could see fleas leaping about the room, when Humphrey strolled into The Secondhand Bookworm carrying an enormous net.

"Sorry I couldn't get here sooner." He apologised. "Guess who I met?"

"Who?"

"Jennifer."

"Oh! Well, I'm pleased." Nora said, surprised.

Humphrey looked annoyed.

Jennifer was Humphrey's ex-fiancé. They had broken up several years earlier when Jennifer had moved to Canada, and then had met by chance at the Halloween Ball in the castle a few weeks ago. Nora had thought the atmosphere between them had sparkled, like the Glitter Angels hosting the ball.

"Yes, well we literally bumped into each other in a hardware shop." Humphrey said, stopping before the counter. "And I had been thinking about what we talked about last night, and about the chemistry between you and the Duke, and I thought you wouldn't mind if I had lunch with her."

Nora smiled.

"No, Humphrey. You seem to like her."

"I do." He admitted and sighed. "But I like you too."

"I like you as well." Nora assured, gazing at him fondly.

"Please don't look at me like that if you don't mean it."

Nora pulled a face and Humphrey laughed.

"So where is this pigeon then, and how on earth did it manage to get into the Bargain Book Yard?" He asked.

"I have no idea how. But he's been sitting on the top of one of the bookcases."

Roger emerged from where he had been in the kitchen making tea. He was carrying two mugs.

"Oh. Fancy a cuppa?" He offered, noticing Humphrey.

"Thanks but no. I've got to get back to work."

"We're just going pigeon catching." Nora said, following Humphrey through the walkway into the backrooms.

"Don't let your tea get cold!"

"No, sir."

Humphrey smirked.

The Bargain Book Yard was full of people. Nora spotted the pigeon peering over the top of a bookcase, as if contemplating pooping on an old man. They approached it slowly, Humphrey holding the net like a burglar. The pigeon stared at them. It was almost within reach so Humphrey lunged at it with a magnificent swing of his net. The pigeon flew into the air, flapped its wings madly, headed for the roof and squeezed between a small gap where the drainpipe from the flats above the Indian Restaurant was located. Nora and Humphrey burst out laughing.

"Maybe I should seal up that area." Humphrey decided.

Nora agreed, both of them chuckling and ignoring the funny looks the bargain hunters were giving them.

Humphrey then placed the large net over Nora.

"Are you still my date for the Thanksgiving dinner tonight?" He asked.

"Why? Would you rather bring Jenny?" She peered at him through the mesh.

"No!" Humphrey frowned.

Nora eased the net from her head and shoulders.

"It should be interesting." She smiled.

"Hmm." Humphrey agreed, following Nora back through the shop to the front.

"Your tea is still hot." Roger pointed out.

"Thanks." Nora appreciated.

"See you both at Georgina's tonight." Humphrey grinned, gave Nora a lingering look and left with his large net.

"There's a rule in fishing." Roger said. "If a fish bites, don't leave it dragging on the hook. Either cut it loose or reel it in."

Nora sighed.

"I know." She agreed.

"And you appear to have two."

Bargain hunters arrived throughout the afternoon, snapping up books from the Bargain Book Yard, haggling over large discounting, clearing shelves, exploring the three floors and six rooms and sending the till into a panic with constant use. Black Friday at The Secondhand Bookworm was a great success. But Nora and Roger were worn out by half past four.

"Do you think Georgina will complain if we leave early?" Roger asked, sipping a fresh hot cup of tea.

"I don't think she will." Nora mused. "She and Troy have been planning this dinner for weeks and they'll want it to be a success."

"I'll throw everyone out soon, then." Roger decided with a menacing gleam in his eye.

Nora noticed through the window that the traffic appeared to have stopped. She decided to investigate. Outside, the air was full of light rain so she bent down, removed the little blue sand pudding weights that stopped the postcard spinners from rolling into the road, wheeled the postcard spinners to the door and hoisted them inside and became aware of an immense sound of yapping, like a pack of dogs.

"Roger! Look!" Nora called, amazed and bemused.

The traffic had indeed stopped up the hill because Billy and Jiao, who ran shops in the antique centres, had somehow managed to let a huge pack of small dogs loose, except the Chihuahua that Jiao carried around in a birdcage.

Nora and Roger stared as Jiao stood on the kerb outside the bank with her Chihuahua in his cage, screaming orders at Billy who was frantically trying to herd what looked like ten Pekinese. It was so comical that Nora doubled up laughing.

The dogs were scampering in all directions. Shop keepers close by had run out of their premises to help. Hugh was running about heavily with a large broom which was frightening the dogs more until finally they were all captured and marshalled into the back of Billy's truck.

"Are they selling Pekinese on the black market?" Roger asked, sipping his tea in the doorway.

"I wouldn't be surprised." Nora giggled as Oliver Braithwaite ran down the hill with two small, snarling dogs in his arms.

Karl pulled up at the kerb, having managed to weave his little Tuk-Tuk through the scampering dogs and blocked cars. He had an old lady as a passenger and beeped his horn at Nora and Roger.

"I almost ran over ten Pekinese." He called from his driver's seat.

"That would have been unfortunate." Nora called back.

"This is Mrs Shinkfield. She's just been up to the Catholic Church for a browse and now would like to visit your Bargain Book Yard." Karl explained, thrusting his thumb back in the direction of his back seats.

Mrs Shinkfield looked like an old hag. She had a musty purple velvet coat, a blouse with what looked like an Elizabethan ruff, and a nose like a beak. Her hair was up inside an ugly purple hat with a small veil. She extended her hand towards Nora and Roger.

Nora and Roger stared.

Nora then nudged Roger's arm.

"Please." Mrs Shinkfield commanded impatiently.

"I think she needs assistance to get out." Nora whispered to Roger.

He sighed and thrust his empty tea mug at Nora.

"Fine." He grumbled.

Karl hunched over his Tuk-Tuk steering wheel, sniggering.

Nora watched as Roger gave Mrs Shinkfield his arm.

"Thank you, young man." She said, which cheered him up considerably. "I hear you have some bargain books."

"You heard correctly, madam." Roger nodded.

She hoisted herself out of the Tuk-Tuk, gripping Roger's forearm so hard that he winced.

"Please show me the way."

"Certainly." Roger agreed and led the old hag past Nora, entering The Secondhand Bookworm.

Karl grinned.

"I'll try and get you some more business." He offered generously.

"Thanks, Karl!" Nora appreciated.

He honked his horn and sped off in the bright orange Tuk-Tuk as the traffic began down the hill once more.

"Got any woodturning books?" A gruff voice asked Nora.

She became aware of a large man at her elbow.

"Oh. Yes, we have a section." She nodded.

"Would that section be in the Bargain Book Yard?" He asked.

"No."

"Damn."

"But our books are all reasonably priced."

"May I have a look? Please and thank you kindly." The man asked.

Nora showed him into the shop where two people were waiting at the counter.

"Oh. Sorry to keep you waiting." Nora apologised.

"Fine."

"Don't worry about it." They mumbled.

"Woodworking is on the top floor in the front room, to the left of the window. We're closing up shortly." Nora explained.

"I won't be long." He assured.

Nora heard him stomping up the stairs like an elephant.

"Sorry to keep you." Nora smiled at the awaiting buyers.

"These are from your Bargain Book Yard." A man with small beady eyes said. He thrust a large pile towards Nora.

"Lovely. Thirty percent off today." She smiled.

"Yeah. Whatever." He rummaged in a man purse for some money.

Nora cleared her throat and rang the prices through the till.

"When is the corn dolly making class?" The man asked.

Nora stared.

"Oh. I'm not sure."

"I've never made corn dollies before." He said and passed Nora a fifty pound note.

"I'm so sorry but I can't take fifty pound notes anymore." Nora apologised.

"What?!"

"We have had several instances of forgeries."

"This is *no* forgery." The man was outraged.

"I'm sorry but this isn't my shop." Nora said warily.

The woman with him picked up a David Bone book to browse.

"Well, that's ridiculous. Humph! Grumph! Humph!"

He sounded like a large animal so Nora wanted to laugh.

"As I said, I am so sorry. Do you have a card?"

"I guess." He said begrudgingly and dug out a credit card.

"Thank you."

Nora hastily did the transaction, bagged up his books and apologised once again. The man stomped off without saying goodbye.

"Sorry about that."

"Oh no, you handled the brute very well. I hate men." The woman said mildly and passed Nora a book about keeping turtles.

"Oh." Nora checked the price and took the sale.

"Thank you, dear. Happy Christmas." The woman bade, shoved the turtle book in her handbag and headed off.

Before anyone else could enter, Nora dived at the door and closed it, placing her key in the lock. She had

had enough of bookworms for the day. She turned the sign to 'CLOSED', checking her watch. It was four fifty.

Roger was still assisting Mrs Shinkfield in the Bargain Book Yard where several other people were gathering large piles of tomes. For some reason, Roger was pleasantly following the old hag around, nodding and fawning over her and holding the books she was pulling out. Nora assumed he was after her fortune.

"I'm going to lock up, Roger." Nora interrupted.

He gave her a frown.

"Oh, are you closing?" A man with armfuls of books asked.

"Yes, in a minute. I'm just going to check upstairs and turn the lights out up there."

"I'll come through in a minute." He nodded.

"Me too."

"Please fetch me that one down." The old hag commanded Roger.

He obeyed.

Bemused, Nora headed off upstairs. She ousted out a young couple smooching in the paperback room, following them down and clearing her throat every time they stopped to kiss on the stairs. No one else was in the shop except the woodworking man who hurried down behind Nora, chatting away about the art of whittling as Nora turned off the lights for upstairs.

It took a good ten minutes for everyone to buy their books and leave, concluding with the old hag who only wanted to deal with Roger. He happily rang her books through the till, bagged them up and carried them to the door where, amazingly, Karl was waiting with the Tuk-Tuk.

Nora glanced at them assisting the old hag into the vehicle while she replied to Cara on the Skype, bid Seatown goodbye and shut down the computer. Roger finally returned.

"I'll lock up the yard and the kitchen." He offered.

"Are you in love?" Nora teased.

"How dare you!" He looked affronted but Nora could see him smirking. "I am just an excellent retailer."

"You go above and beyond."

"Thank you. Despite your mockery." Roger said and headed off to the back.

Nora grinned at the large amount of money they had taken again that day. She counted out the float, turned off the till and shrugged into her coat.

"I'll just use the gender fluid restroom." Roger decided.

Nora handed him the loo keys and waited impatiently for him, watching a group of boys in the dusky town square kicking an empty can of coke around until Hugh descended like a monster and frightened them away.

Finally, Roger returned and after putting on heaps of layers he set the alarm, turned off the lights and they left.

"Thank you for your pleasing company, today." Roger said.

"You're welcome." Nora replied.

He glowered.

"Oh…thank you for your charming company." She added.

"That's better." He said.

"See you later." Nora grinned.

"See you later." Roger smiled, they parted, and Nora set off up the hill to get ready for her first ever Thanksgiving Dinner.

Georgina Pickering lived in a large house on the outskirts of Piertown. She was currently sharing the house with her American boyfriend, Troy. Humphrey was living there too and Mrs Pickering, Georgina and Humphrey's mother, had recently moved into an annex attached to the large house.

Several cars were parked along the street outside the driveway and on the semi-circular drive, belonging to the staff of The Secondhand Bookworm. Nora parked her Smart Car behind Betty's new white IQ, turned off the engine and almost screamed.

Her driver's door was opening by itself.

"Humphrey!" Nora rebuked when his grinning face leaned in.

"Mademoiselle?" He laughed, offering her his arm.

"You almost gave me a heart attack."

Nora climbed out and straightened up in front of him. He looked smart in a grey Chambray shirt with navy blue trousers.

"I was waiting for you. Georgina and Troy are driving me mad." He said.

Nora chuckled.

"Oh dear."

He kissed her cheek.

"You smell nice. And you look lovely." He complimented.

"Thanks. So do you." Nora returned.

Humphrey waited for her to lock her car and then they walked up the drive.

"There are a lot of alcoholic beverages laid out. Georgina has prepared four guest bedrooms for people who get tipsy and want to stay." Humphrey explained.

"Sounds fun." Nora said.

"How was the bookshop today, after the pigeon?"

Nora told Humphrey all the events that had occurred so that he was doubled up laughing as they stepped into Georgina's large entrance hall.

"Good evening, Nora!" Georgina greeted, swishing towards her in a beautiful red silk gown.

"Oh. Georgina you look lovely. Should I have dressed up more?" Nora asked, finding herself squished in a tight embrace.

"No. Troy's driving me crazy." Georgina murmured in Nora's ear.

Nora arched an eyebrow.

"Can I help?"

"Oh, he just wants everything to go perfectly tonight. Americans." Georgina waved off and helped Nora out of her coat. "People are having drinks in the lounge."

"Where are the dogs?"

"The dogs?! Can you imagine them bowling everyone over with excitement? They're in the annex for the evening. Fluffy is about somewhere." Georgina said, referring to her cat. She took hold of Nora's hand and practically dragged her into the lounge.

Nora glanced back at Humphrey who smirked.

Georgina's lounge was enormous. There were huge paintings of beautiful faced women about the walls and a real full-sized suit of armour next to the fireplace.

"Nora!" Cara, Heather and Felix greeted as she was steered in.

"Hello everyone." Nora smiled, glancing at the bookworms seated in various huge sofas, chairs or standing mingling. It seemed as though everyone was there so Nora had been the last to arrive.

"I am sure you recognise the music." Georgina said.

Heather waved her hand at Nora and pointed to herself.

"Oh. Yes I do!" Nora nodded, recognising her sister's piano compositions.

"Heather brought it with her and I've fallen in love with it." Georgina gushed.

"Drink, Nora?" Humphrey offered, indicating to what seemed to be the entire drink contents of a pub.

"Thank you. My usual, please." She smiled.

He headed off to pour her a gin and tonic, joining Cal and Seymour who were sampling tipples.

"HONEYCAKES!!!" Troy's voice yelled from the direction of the kitchen, using his pet name for Georgina.

"Oh. I'd better go and see what he wants." Georgina smiled and rustled off.

Everyone exchanged smirks.

"I'm starving." Cara admitted as Nora joined her on one of the humungous red sofas.

"It smells delicious."

"Potluck style turkey." Mrs Pickering said, sipping a prosecco.

Humphrey brought Nora's drink over to her and squashed next to her.

"Troy has games lined up for after dinner." He said.

"What games?" Roger looked up from browsing one of the coffee table books about the oceans of the world.

"You'll see." Humphrey smirked.

Roger glowered.

"And we're watching the Macey's Thanksgiving Day Parade." Betty said. "Troy recorded it from this morning in New York City."

"What?" Nora was bemused.

"It's what they do in America." Heather said.

"It's three hours long." Humphrey murmured in Nora's ear.

She almost choked on her gin and tonic.

Georgina reappeared.

"Dinner will be served shortly. Please make your way into the dining room." She announced, holding a glass of sherry and looking stressed.

Everyone stood up or left the drinks table and walked out of the lounge.

"Have you seen Georgina's miniature book collection?" Cara asked Heather as they passed a carved walnut bookcase in the hall.

"No. Oh, how amazing!" Heather exclaimed.

The rest of the bookshop party entered the dining room which was large and formal and now a breath-taking sight.

The room had been decorated for Thanksgiving, with the large, long twelve-seater table covered in a tablecloth that had '*Thanksgiving*' printed over it in red script. Bouquets of autumn flowers had been displayed around orange candles and there was a cornucopia as a centrepiece. Decorations included dolls of pilgrims and turkeys and decorated gourds, displayed on sideboards around the room. There were already delicious smelling dishes of food, covered, and placed along the whole table.

The places had name settings so everyone found their own and took their seats. Troy and Georgina were at the head and foot of the table. Mrs Pickering and Roger were opposite one another by Georgina (Cara whispered that she thought Georgina was trying to set them up); Felix and Heather were next, opposite each other, followed by Cal and Betty, Nora and Humphrey and finally Cara and Seymour near Troy.

Troy and Georgina arrived. Troy was carrying an enormous turkey and Georgina a ham. Everyone clapped.

"Before I begin to carve the turkey," Troy announced, standing at his place, "we will join hands and go around the table, taking it in turns to say what we are thankful for."

Everyone looked a mixture of wary, worried or angry (Roger the latter).

Troy sat down and took Cara and Seymour's hands. Seymour and Nora held hands and Cal took hold of Nora's right hand. They soon all felt a little silly but smiled around as Troy began.

"I am thankful for meeting Georgina, the love of my life, and for sharing this meal with you all." He said.

Everyone thought that was really lovely and there were several 'ahhh's and ooooh's'.

Cara cleared her throat.

"I am thankful for being invited here this evening, for my job and for my husband." She said.

Seymour winked at her.

Felix pretended to silently vomit.

Humphrey was next.

"I am thankful for not being pooped upon by the pigeon in the Bargain Book Yard this afternoon." He said.

"Humphrey!" Georgina rebuked while several people laughed.

He shrugged, winking at Nora.

Everyone offered thanks for various things and people, including Felix completing his latest Nintendo game, which he swore was incredibly hard, Betty meeting a deliciously wicked man today and Nora thanking their hosts and saying she was thankful for knowing everyone. Seymour thanked Jesus for the meal and then Troy began to carve the turkey.

There were sweet potatoes, cornbread, vegetables, gravy, mashed potatoes and the turkey was stuffed with bread and celery. It was a veritable feast and the wine poured in abundance.

At one point, Fluffy snuck in so Cara and Nora slipped little pieces of turkey to him under the table. Troy told some amusing and interesting stories about his life in America and eventful Thanksgiving meals he had celebrated, as well as a history of the Puritans and Pilgrims who emigrated from England in the 1620s and 1630s to America.

When everyone had eaten the main meal, the table was cleared and desserts arrived. Large selections of pies were set along the centre including apple, pecan, cherry and pumpkin. Georgina and Troy dished up and then

Georgina began to make additional 'thankful' toasts which were peppered with hiccups and gulps of wine.

"And I am of course thankful to Felix for not buggering up the large sale I trusted him with on Saturday. He did so well!" Georgina toasted, causing Cara to choke with laughter and Felix to gaze around, mildly offended.

"I am thankful for you all, my lovelies, my darling shop workers. And that is why I am pleased to announce, hiccup…"

Everyone looked at her in curious expectation as to what she was going to announce.

"That…hiccup…it is with joy…tee-hee…that I announce that Troy and I shall be immigrating to America next year!"

Everyone stared.

Nora stopped chewing, Cara looked at Nora and grinned and Betty gasped.

"Oh Georgina how lovely for you! Congratulations!" Betty toasted.

"Thank you, thank you. Ah as you know, Troy and I are madly in love," Georgina continued dreamily, "and I have been in meetings with Nora and Cara who have agreed to buy The Secondhand Bookworms from me."

Everyone clapped.

"You're going to sell the shops?" Felix was amazed.

"Yes, Felix honey, but don't worry, all your jobs are safe. Nora and Cara will be running The Secondhand Bookworms as usual, in a business partnership together."

Nora shook her head at Felix teasingly. He grinned. She reached for her glass, hiding her surprise about the sudden announcement and the reality that Georgina was planning to leave next year behind a large swig of prosecco.

Humphrey gave her an encouraging smile so she smiled back at him.

Georgina and Troy's future was the topic of conversation for the rest of the meal until they retired to the lounge and Troy turned on the Macey's Thanksgiving Day parade, telling them with pride that it was the largest parade in the world.

Nora found herself snuggled next to Humphrey on one of the sofas and enjoyed watching the floats, marching bands, cheerleaders, falloons, balloonicles, enormous balloons managed by ninety people each, casts of the shows currently on Broadway and lots of songs.

Roger left halfway through but everyone else stayed. Heather and Cara fell asleep, Betty got very drunk and Mrs Pickering went to bed, releasing Chubby and Rufus, Georgina's two huge Leonberger dogs, from her annex. They bounded in and almost licked everyone to death before settling down.

After Santa arrived to ring in the Christmas shopping season in New York City, Troy put on a football match and made them all play Yahtzee until Seymour and Cara retired to one of the guest rooms, Betty to another, Heather and Felix left, Cal bagsied another guest room, Georgina and Troy went off to bed and Nora and Humphrey remained chatting and laughing on their own in the lounge after a very long and very entertaining Thanksgiving Dinner celebration.

9 BLACK FRIDAY

"Good morning, sleepy heads!"

Nora sat bolt upright, accidently elbowing Humphrey in the stomach next to her so that he yelled out.

"Owwwww!"

"Where am I?"

Georgina was grinning at them in her lounge, wearing a silk pink dressing gown with, amazingly, her hair in curlers.

"You're in my lounge, Nora." She laughed.

Nora blinked and looked around.

"Oh my." She said and fell back next to Humphrey who was rubbing his stomach.

"I'm making a cooked breakfast for everyone in the kitchen."

"Thanks." Humphrey nodded, smirking at Nora who gave him an apologetic grin.

"Ready in five minutes." Georgina sang, heading off.

She was replaced by Chubby who lunged at them excitably.

"I don't remember falling asleep." Nora admitted, yawning and stroking Chubby who decided to go and visit someone else and left the lounge.

"You were in the middle of singing 'Just Eat it!' by Weird Al Yankovic to me and you suddenly went unconscious." Humphrey said.

Nora burst out laughing.

"Have some more chicken
Have some more pie
It doesn't matter
If it's boiled or fried
Just eat it, just eat it
Just eat it, just eat it, Woo!" She sang, remembering, and she and Humphrey doubled over laughing.

"Ow. Ugh. I need a shower." Nora grimaced.

"Have breakfast first." Humphrey hoped.

"I won't say no." Nora agreed with a smile. "But I must use the ladies room."

Humphrey watched her go, grinning, so she rolled her eyes and used the downstairs restroom, freshening up, tidying her hair and then making her way to the large kitchen. Cara, Seymour, Cal and Betty were already tucking in to a large cooked breakfast around a big rustic table.

Humphrey appeared in a fresh white t-shirt and pulled out a chair for Nora at the breakfast table.

"Black Friday today ladies!" Georgina said cheerfully, dishing up fried tomatoes.

Nora checked her watch.

"It's only seven thirty!" She exclaimed.

"Plenty of time to eat, go home, shower and change and open up for Black Friday!" Georgina smiled happily.

Nora was distracted by Georgina's curlers. Cara noticed and sniggered.

"Oh Nora I do hope you have a good day in takings." Betty said through a mouthful of bread.

"There's not *mush-room* on this plate." Humphrey said, waiting for Georgina to add fried mushrooms to his hash browns, eggs, sausages, beans and bacon.

Nora giggled.

"Mush-room? As in – much room?" Seymour realised and laughed, shaking his head.

"I'm working with Cara today so I'm sure we will." Nora grinned, nodding a thank you to Georgina serving her food.

"Can I come with you and use the shower in your place?" Cara asked, taking a swig of tea.

"Sure." Nora nodded.

"I think I have some jeans at your flat."

"You have. I ironed them the other evening."

"Thanks!" Cara appreciated.

"Can I bring my ironing around to yours?" Cal joked.

Everyone laughed.

Troy joined them all for breakfast, complimenting their appetites and admiring the amount they were demolishing after the Thanksgiving dinner.

"We're going to Horsham and then on to Lewis, looking at libraries of books today, with a few small calls." Georgina explained.

"Please no." Nora lamented.

"I'm building up a good stock for you for when I hand over the business next year." Georgina smiled.

"We'll have nowhere to put it all." Cara mused.

"Oh it'll be sold long before then." Seymour said.

Everyone looked at him.

"What?" He shrugged, cramming a mouthful of sausage in. "Cara talks book trade even in her sleep."

"Do I?" Cara asked.

Seymour smirked.

"Nora sings in her sleep." Humphrey said.

Everyone looked at him. And then at Nora.

"Just to clarify, we fell asleep on the sofa last night." Nora explained, giving Humphrey a look.

"Wishful thinking, mate." Seymour said, nudging Humphrey's elbow.

Nora went red and hastily ate up her meal.

After breakfast, everyone thanked Georgina and Troy once more, offered to clean up but Georgina said her house cleaner was due in at nine and that she should earn her money. Betty was dropping Cal to his flat in Seatown so they set off, followed by Nora and Cara. Seymour headed off to his theatre in Little Cove and Humphrey went off for a shower.

Castletown was quiet and misty as Nora reversed into a space not far from her flat. There was an hour and a half until opening time so Nora and Cara took it in turns to use Nora's shower. Nora lent Cara one of her clean and ironed 'The Secondhand Bookworm' work blouses, they did each other's hair into waterfall braids, played with Beardie, listened to music and then did some small weight lifting along to a 1980's exercise video Nora had found in a box of books Georgina had dropped in.

Still laughing about the video, the two women walked down to The Secondhand Bookworm and stared in amazement at a long queue that had formed outside the bookshop.

"Oh! Good morning." Nora greeted, taking out her keys.

"Morning." A rotund man said.

"Are you opening soon?" A woman asked from behind him.

"Give us just a moment to turn on the lights for you and open the Bargain Book Yard at the back of the shop, madam." Cara said.

"Yes, the Bargain Book Yard. That's what we're here for!" People chorused.

The other shop keepers were staring as they pretended to examine their window displays or sweep their doorsteps. Phil and Alice from the delicatessen were standing in their doorway, watching with amazement while Tim and Sam, the butcher brothers, were carrying whole pig carcasses across the square from a van, grinning at them. Nora unlocked and Cara ran in to turn off the alarm.

"Two minutes, sir." Nora said, stopping the rotund man from barging in.

"Hurry up about it." He said, salivating.

Nora grimaced, locked the door behind her and ran across the carpet.

"That man was drooling in anticipation."

"It's going to be a *cwazy* day." Cara grinned.

"I'll turn the lights on and open the kitchen and yard." Nora said, throwing her bag under the stairs.

"I'll fill up the till. Yikes. It's like Shawn of the Dead." Cara pointed.

People were gathered around the door and the windows, pressing their faces against the glass, pointing and peering in as if wanting to devour the books.

Nora laughed, grabbed the keys and ran off.

The Bargain Book Yard was ready for destruction. Nora had turned on the pumpkin face lights, wedged open the kitchen door and heard Cara call through to her that she was opening the door to the zombies.

"Okay!" Nora called back and put the kettle on for tea.

She was a bit hung over from drinking all the alcoholic beverages that Georgina had plied her with at the Thanksgiving dinner and intended to just remain behind the counter and serve the Black Friday bargain hunters that day. She was sure that would be exhausting enough.

Voices were growing closer so Nora squashed herself against the worktops holding the milk as a crowd of people jostled and hurried into the Bargain Book Yard. She watched as handfuls of books were grabbed, people were pushing and a man was flailing his arms in an attempt to have the sci-fi section all to himself.

Quickly, Nora made two mugs of tea before hurrying out the front.

"Seymour picked up Arthur and is keeping him with him for the day at the theatre." Cara said, holding up her iPhone.

Nora chuckled at a photo of Arthur in his red jumper with a white bone on the front, sitting in the front row seats of the Jolly Theatre next to Seymour as he watched some auditions. Seymour owned the popular Art Deco theatre just outside of Little Cove and drew many crowds to the plays he put on there.

"Your phone was ringing." Cara then added.

"Probably Humphrey." Nora sighed.

"What is it with you two? He's obsessed." Cara grinned.

"Hmm." Nora waved her hand in dismissal, rummaging for her phone in her bag. "Oh, I'll put the poster up for today, the one that says 'BLACK FRIDAY BARGAIN BOOK YARD SALE – FIFTY PERCENT OFF TODAY!'"

"Okay." Cara nodded, rummaging for it.

The phone call had been spam so Nora shoved her iPhone in the pocket of her jeans and organised the posters in the window. She and Cara then put out the bargain book trolley, the postcard spinners, the cheap paperback boxes and the box of free maps as more people arrived.

"Look at the Woman in Gold!" Cara exclaimed.

Nora stared.

The Woman in Gold was wearing a Chewbacca mask and a Sith Lord robe from the Star Wars movies. It looked hilarious. They both then spotted Harry jogging towards them and didn't have a chance to dive into the shop for cover.

"Hiiiiiiiii." Harry greeted smoothly, sticking his chest out and running on the spot when he reached them.

"Morning, Harry." Nora returned.

"Hiiiii Harry." Cara grinned.

"How's the ice rink?" Nora asked.

"Great. Fancy coming for a private skate after hours? Just you and me?" He asked hopefully.

"No." Nora said.

"Fair enough." Harry smiled.

A knot of people attempted to enter the shop, almost pushing Harry into the road in front of a bus. Nora grabbed his arm and pulled him back onto the kerb.

"You saved my life." He ogled.

"No problem." Nora cleared her throat.

"No I owe you." Harry grinned and winked.

Nora wiped her hand on her trousers from his sweaty arm and grimaced.

Cara giggled, watching Harry jog off while glancing back at Nora.

"You just made a bad situation worse." Cara smirked.

"I should have let him get flattened by the bus." Nora lamented, following a swarm of bargain hunters into The Secondhand Bookworm.

There was a queue at the till so Cara ran around to take the sales. Nora spent the next half an hour answering questions, directing people and showing customers the prices in books in the Bargain Book Yard. It was manic. Finally, at half past eleven there was a lull as everyone went off to have a cup of tea. Nora and Cara's tea was cold so Nora microwaved them both.

When she came back to the front, Cara was madly clicking the mouse while staring at the computer screen.

"Look! I just bought the whole series of 'Bones' on DVD from Amazon. There are some amazing Black Friday deals." Cara exclaimed.

Nora laughed.

"Careful." She warned.

"I know. It's so tempting. Seymour says I can buy three box sets, no more."

Nora smirked.

Several more people arrived asking for the Bargain Books, so Nora took a quick sip of her tea and showed them the way to the Bargain Book Yard.

"Just through here…" She directed and stopped dead.

A large clanking and clattering sound was coming from inside the Bargain Book Yard. The black and white bunting was flapping wildly around, the pumpkin face lights were jiggling up and down and several posters were flapping about the room. A man browsing the books was holding onto his hat.

"Oh what a lovely room!" One of the ladies Nora had directed admired.

Nora realised that the estate agents had turned the air conditioning unit on and that was the cause of the racket and the cyclone.

"Oh…my." Nora muttered, turned around and hurried back to Cara.

"I just bought the whole 'Stargate: SG1' series!" Cara said triumphantly.

"The estate agents have turned on the air conditioning!" Nora replied.

"What?!" Cara stared.

"I'll have to go round and ask them to turn it off. Our bargain hunters are being blown about the room."

Nora left Cara sniggering into her tea and set off out the shop. She peered into the window of the estate agents next door as she passed and could see the three ladies sitting at their desks. One of them was polishing her fingernails.

Grateful that they didn't have any clients, Nora knocked on the door, opened it and stepped down into the bright, boring looking room.

"Oh. Hello!" One lady greeted.

"Hello. I'm from the bookshop next door." Nora said and choked on the overwhelming scents of perfume.

"Oh hello. Yes, I recognise you." The first lady said, fluffing up her hair with a wide toothed comb. "I'm Kelly."

"I'm Nora. I'm afraid your air conditioning unit is on and blowing loud air around our book yard."

Kelly gasped.

"Is it!? I'm so sorry." She apologised, looking across at her colleagues.

"I turned it on. Wasn't I supposed to?" A slender woman with blond hair, heavy make-up and a lace blouse asked.

"No. Not until next week."

"Why did you turn it on, Candice?" The third lady tittered. "It's November."

"I was hot, Charlotte."

"Please turn it off, Candice. We have an agreement with our neighbours." Kelly said.

"If you insist." Candice sighed, stood up, looked down her perfect nose at Nora and clip-clopped off in needle-thin stilettos to the controller.

"Thank you so much." Nora appreciated.

"Apologies once again." Kelly said.

"Thank you. We only need it off until Monday."

"Yes. Georgina told me. Have a good day."

"Oh…erm…bye." Nora said and made a hasty escape.

Out on the street, Nora noticed the people from the antique shop on the other side of The Secondhand Bookworm carrying boxes of tools and sheets of wood into their shop. She sighed, expecting banging and crashing to accompany them that afternoon.

When she stepped down into the bookshop, Nora grimaced to see Miss Raven standing at the counter speaking to Cara. She wore her usual large white duffle coat, pink flannel shorts, white plimsolls, knee high socks and deer hunter hat. Her voice was high and passive aggressive.

"As you know, we are very good customers, loyal and faithful, and mother has found several books out there that we would like."

"I'm sorry, but I can't give an extra ten percent off when I do fifty percent. That would be sixty percent off." Cara said with a forced smile.

Nora cleared her throat.

"Hello Miss Raven."

Miss Raven turned. She smiled sweetly.

"Hello. Did you ask Georgina about our special discount?"

"I'm afraid my colleague is right. We can't do sixty percent off for you." Nora apologised warily.

Miss Raven's blue eyes snapped. Her lips became a very small, tight smile.

"I see."

"It's a very good deal to have fifty percent off." Nora added charmingly.

"Yes, it is. But it is the same as what everyone is getting off, and we are valued customers." Miss Raven hissed.

"I'm so sorry." Nora apologised again.

"We may have to leave the books." Miss Raven said.

"Oh dear. I'm sorry to hear that."

"It would be nice to be treated as valuable customers."

Nora and Cara just smiled politely.

At that moment, Mrs Raven shuffled in from the Bargain Book Yard, huffing and puffing as she carried a small pile of books.

"Did you…did you…did you ask her if…did you…?" She wheezed.

"YES Poppet!" Miss Raven snapped and led her mother into a corner by the art books where they put their heads together and huddled over their book choices, whispering.

"Ahem." Nora said.

Cara rolled her eyes.

At that moment, Crossword- Lady arrived, carrying her morning paper.

Nora stifled a groan.

"Hello, Gina." Crossword-Lady greeted.

"Hello." Nora smiled tightly.

"Congratulations again on your new movie role. Yes, I would like to be a part of it. Where can I sign up?"

Nora and Cara stared blankly.

"Pardon?"

"The Book Club movie role we spoke about earlier in the week. I took a flyer and would like to help you with your research. Will we be reading porn?"

Cara choked on her tea.

Nora tried not to laugh.

"Oh. You mean the Book Club here. No, we won't. We will be studying a series of novels that have been privately printed." She explained.

"Oh. Intriguing. Count me in."

Nora was silent a long moment before resigning herself to Crossword-Lady being a part of the club.

"Okay. Thank you. That would be very nice." She rummaged around for her list under the counter.

Crossword-Lady smiled dreamily, waiting.

"We will be meeting here every Thursday evening from six o'clock until eight thirty with sandwiches, tea and cake provided. You can collect your copy of the first book from tomorrow and the first meeting takes place on Thursday 14th December so you will need to have read it and finished it by then. The Book Club runs for seven weeks."

"Sounds marvellous." Crossword-Lady said and took the form to write her name and number.

Miss Raven glided over.

"I couldn't help but overhear. Are you having a Book Club?" She asked.

Nora couldn't believe it.

"Erm…yes, we are."

"Are they children's books?"

"No, sorry." Nora assured, relieved.

"Then I think I would like to join. I've wanted to broaden my horizons and this will be a good place to start."

"Oh how lovely. Here, sign your name under mine." Crossword-Lady said, passing Miss Raven the sheet of paper.

"Thank you." Miss Raven nodded.

Nora and Cara looked at one another. Cara looked amused. Nora looked aghast.

"Ask her if…ask her if…" Mrs Raven's whispering drew closer, accompanied by huffing and puffing like a steam train.

"I WILL Poppet!" Miss Raven said, concentrating.

When Miss Raven had handed back the form, Nora wrote the dates and instructions on the back of one of her flyers and gave it to her. Miss Raven looked pleased.

"Now, about these books." She snatched the pile from her mother who was staring at Nora.

"As I said…"

"We would be happy to take them with a fifty percent discount." Miss Raven interrupted firmly, with flashing eyes.

"Oh." Nora said.

"Please could you bag each one up separately? They are heavy after all."

Nora took the books. There were three and they were just pathetic flimsy children's books with hardly any pages.

"No problem." She humoured and she and Cara rang the sale through.

Mrs Raven opened a crumpled bank bag for coins and counted out tiny five pence pieces and ten pence pieces so as to pay. Nora bagged each book up separately while muttering insults under her breath that only Cara could hear so that Cara laughed so much she began to choke.

"I look forward to seeing you at the Book Club." Crossword-Lady smiled at Miss Raven as the Ravens gathered up their enormous pile of bags and carrier bags they had dumped behind the counter.

"Pardon?" Miss Raven demanded.

"I said I look forward to seeing you at the Book Club." Crossword-Lady patiently repeated.

The phone began to ring so both Nora and Cara dove for it in the hope of being freed from the Ravens and Crossword-Lady. Cara grabbed it first and answered it with a triumphant grin. Which then faded.

"Oh. Hello, Mr Hill."

"Ha-ha-ha!" Nora pointed.

Cara stuck her tongue out.

"Yes, we can see if we have those in stock." Cara said.

Nora knew that Mr Hill, who had sold his books in the Seatown branch earlier that week, was now making plans to buy them back. The insane marathon of buying and selling his same fifteen books for the past several decades continued.

"I can have them sent over here for tomorrow if you like." Cara said, grinning at Nora.

Nora gasped.

"Oh, okay yes I understand. Oh, how lovely." Cara scowled.

"Goodbye, Gina. I shall pop in next week to collect my copy of our first book. Are you sure it's not porn." Crossword-Lady asked as the Ravens departed with whispers and immense rustling of bags.

"It certainly is not!" Nora assured.

"While I'm here, I have this literary clue, as long as you don't cheat."

Nora sighed.

"Of course. What's the question today?"

"(Blank) Wake by James Joyce. One of the most difficult works in the English language." Crossword-Lady said.

"Finnegans." Nora answered. "Finnegans Wake."

"Oh, yes that should fit. I've never heard of it." Crossword-Lady admitted, picking up a pen.

"Well, it certainly is one of the most difficult books to read in the English language." Nora said.

Crossword-Lady smiled, filling in her crossword.

"Thank you, Gina. I look forward to the Book Club." She said, turned and headed off.

Cara hung up from speaking with Mr Hill.

"He's coming into Seatown tomorrow. I might get Cal to deal with him." She smirked.

Nora laughed.

"Excuse me! Have you got any new books?" A man with purple glasses asked.

"We have a few." Cara replied.

"By the way, your plants need watering."

"We don't have any plants." Nora said, confused.

"In the Bargain Book Yard. Lots of plants out there." The man nodded.

"Hello? Have you got any cheaper postcards?" An old lady called in from the doorway.

Nora was still puzzling over what plants they had in the Bargain Book Yard. She concluded he meant the tiny weeds poking through the paving slabs.

"Do you sell chocolate?" The man about the plants asked.

Nora decided he was just crazy.

"No, sorry."

Throngs of people emerged from the back of the shop carrying heaps of books. Cara got up to deal with the postcard lady, leaving Nora to sell lots of books, write down the amounts and answer the telephone.

"Hello!"

A lady with long blond hair stood at the counter smiling.

"Hello." Nora smiled back.

"I work in a restaurant down Market Street but we have to close in the New Year." She said.

"Oh, I'm sorry to hear that."

"Hmm, yes, the restaurant business can be tough. I was wondering if you have any part-time work."

"For the New Year?"

"Well, I can start soon. My partner Christopher will be working in the restaurant until it closes but I'm looking for new things now. I'm Amy by the way. You might remember my daughter, Henrietta. She worked here on weekends until she went to live with her dad in Canada. And Charlene, her half-sister, worked here before that."

"Oh! Yes, I remember Henri and Charlie." Nora nodded. "You're Henrietta's mum."

"Yes." Amy grinned.

"Nice to meet you. I'm Nora. If you leave your mobile number I'll pass it on to Georgina. She's the owner and the one to talk to about jobs."

"Thank you. That'd be great." Amy said, grabbed a pen and scribbled down her number.

"I'll make sure she gets it." Nora smiled.

"Thanks. Bye, Nora."

Nora said goodbye, watching Amy set off cheerfully.

"Have you got a train timetable?" A man asked.

He had a glum face and his hair was sticking up really high on his head. He reminded Nora of a sad leek.

"I'm afraid we don't." She assured.

Immense banging and crashing sounded from next door. Work had started up in the antique shop. Nora sighed.

When Cara came back in from outside Nora decided to go and check on the Bargain Book Yard and make some tea. She stopped in the back room to tidy some shelves and then stepped into the yard. Her eyes popped.

Most of the shelves had been stripped! The remaining books now looked incredibly messed up, higgledy-piggledy in piles on the shelves, or lying on their sides, or even discarded in heaps on the floor. The three tables were in chaos. At least five people were rummaging and two of them looked aggressive and frantic. Nora decided that bargain book hunters were scary.

She turned around and put the kettle on for tea, jumping at the sounds of books falling from the shelves or off the tables.

By the time she returned to the front of the shop, Cara had added up the sales and announced that they had just gone over a thousand pounds.

"Unbelievable." Nora gazed, sitting down on the rickety old stool to sip her tea.

"How is it in the yard?"

"Go and see for yourself. It's the pits."

"I think I'll leave it." Cara decided. "Or I'll be tempted to tidy up."

"I don't think we'll have many books left out there at the end of the day."

"Aren't we having a big sale tomorrow as well?"

"Yes. Georgina is expecting it to be busy because of the farmer's market in the square so she has asked Heather to work here with me and Felix."

"Maybe we should put more books out there?"

"Hmm. We pretty much cleared the shop of bargain books."

"How about any from that pile?"

They both looked at the mounds in front of the window.

"We could mark them up at twice the price and people will think they're getting fifty percent off." Cara giggled. "And they get free fleas too."

Nora sniggered.

"That's tempting. What about if I ask if Georgina has any ideas? Even if we just put a load of books on the shelves without them being in order it would be good. People seem to just be rummaging randomly anyway."

"Give her a call."

"Alright." Nora nodded and picked up the shop phone. She dialled Georgina's number and a moment later Georgina answered.

"Everything alright?" Her sing-song voice asked.

"Yes and no."

"What's happened?"

Nora stepped back and moved to under the stairs as more people came to the till to buy bargain books. Cara dealt with the sales.

"We're running out of books in the Bargain Book Yard!" Nora whispered down the phone.

"Really?!" Georgina laughed. "Well we can't have that! Troy and I are on our way back from Horsham. We bought a whole library as a job lot and there's some tat included. We'll come now and pull out some boxfuls from the back of the van for your yard."

"Oh that's brilliant!" Nora appreciated.

"See you in a bit!"

Nora relayed the information to Cara who looked pleased.

"I'll see how they're doing in Seatown. We have so many bargain books in the temporary annex there and they're not going as well as they are here. We could get Roger and Paperback Pam to box some up and maybe Humphrey will bring them over too."

"I'm sure Georgina would agree. She won't want cheap books hanging around after Black Friday finishes."

Cara jumped onto the Skype and asked how things were going with the bargain books.

'*Slow.*' Roger replied.

'*Are the shelves still full? And are there boxes of books still to go on them out there? Please check. Waiting.*'

'*Alright Mein Führer!*' Roger wrote back.

Cara glowered. Nora giggled.

"He doesn't like taking orders from me. Wait until we're his bosses." Cara said smugly.

"I wonder how he's getting on with Paperback Pam." Nora pondered.

Cara smirked.

A moment later Roger told them that there were four boxes still to go out and that the shelves in the sale annex were modestly full. They had been selling some cheap books but Black Friday in Seatown seemed to only be drawing the crowds to the electrical shops rather than The Secondhand Bookworm.

"That figures." Nora ruminated.

"Why don't you ask if Humphrey will pop into Seatown and pick up the boxes and bring them here?" Cara suggested. "I'll tell Roger to fill up four more boxes from the shelves so there will be eight for Humphrey to collect. We're not going to shift them all from Seatown tomorrow. Best to have the Bargain Book Yard here full up."

"I like that plan." Nora nodded and dug out her iPhone.

When she lifted it she noticed she already had a text and her heart gave a small flutter when she saw that it was from the Duke of Cole. Quickly, Nora opened it and read:

'Good morning. How are things today? – James'

Nora stared.

The Bargain Book Yard was forgotten as she sat down to reply, leaving Cara typing a bossy Skype message to Roger.

'Good morning. Busy here today in the shop for Black Friday. Shelves are being stripped so we're organising more stock. How are you?' She wrote and pressed send.

A moment later.

'Glad to hear the bookshop is doing well. Currently overseeing the changing of four hundred lightbulbs.'

Nora laughed.

Cara turned and looked at her.

"Is he coming?" She asked.

"What? Oh." Nora went red. "I haven't asked him yet."

Another message arrived.

'When can I see you again?' The Duke had written.

Nora looked down and went even redder.

'I'd like to pop down and pick up the first book for the Book Club (and see you).' Another message said.

Nora replied quickly.

'I'd like to see you too. I'll have your copy under the counter. It would be lovely if you popped in.'

Cara was staring at Nora, curious. She then turned back to the Skype and gasped.

"Roger's now calling me *Dictador Perpetuo*!" Cara read.

Nora laughed.

'I'll be in this afternoon, Nora. See you soon x' The Duke replied.

Nora almost fell off the stool when she read the 'x'. It was the first 'x' sent between them. She stared at it for ages, grinning stupidly.

"Nora. I said, have you asked Humphrey yet?" Cara repeated, bemused.

Nora turned her iPhone to face Cara.

"The Duke just sent me an 'x'." She whispered hard.

Cara's eyes popped.

"Really?! You're texting with the Duke?! Let me see!" Cara grabbed Nora's phone and stared too. She then scrolled back up the messages, reading them. "OM golly-gosh!" Cara grinned, delighted. "I knew he liked you. He likes you *lots*!"

"He may have just been being friendly." Nora decided.

"That was a calculated 'x'. Send him an 'x' back." Cara demanded.

Nora laughed.

"No!"

"But he's a Duke! You need to let him know the 'x' is mutual."

"I don't care about his Dukedom. I actually like him for who he is."

"True love." Cara sighed dreamily.

"Shush!" Nora laughed and shook her head. "Look, I need to go and get him his copy of 'The Missing Candlesticks' for the Book Club. Shall I go now?"

"Can you bring my copy down too, please?" Cara asked eagerly.

"Yes, I'll bring a pile down. People will be popping in for them for the Book Club now. Do you mind?"

"No. Go ahead. Oooh. The Duke's going to be paying you a visit this afternoon. He he he. Can I tell Seymour?"

"No." Nora said.

Cara pouted.

"Poor Humphrey." She then sympathised.

"It's not like I'm going on a date with the Duke, Cara!" Nora assured in a low voice.

"Yet!" Cara grinned and turned as another Skype arrived.

'As long as I'm not wasting my time. We are rather busy here!' Roger had written.

"Honestly. I'm going to suspend him." Cara decided, glowering.

Laughing, Nora grabbed her coat and set off out The Secondhand Bookworm for her flat, unable to help but grin at the thought of the Duke's impending visit.

10 THE INCREDIBLE SALE

Nora returned to The Secondhand Bookworm carrying a small box full of copies of volume one in her Book Club novels, having spoken with Humphrey and organised for him to pick up the eight boxes of bargain books from Seatown. As she approached she saw that the bookshop van had arrived.

Troy and Georgina were rummaging in the back of the van which was parked outside the antique shop next door, with boxes and crates on the path and on part of the road beside them. Books were being placed inside as they sorted through the tomes that would be suitable for the Bargain Book Yard.

"Ah, hello Nora!" Georgina greeted cheerfully.

"Hiya Nora." Troy grinned.

"Hi. Sorry to interrupt your calls."

"No worries. We need to have a lunch break anyway before the next few." Georgina assured.

"Wow. You've filled up the van." Nora noticed.

"Yes, so this is a good thing. We'll have room to buy more books now." Georgina laughed. "I bought some very interesting books about mountaineering. A whole specialist library with some very rare volumes."

Nora's ears pricked up.

"Really? Do you have them with you?"

"Yes. In a couple of boxes at the front."

Nora lowered her voice.

"The Duke of Cole is coming in to see me this afternoon. He may be interested."

Georgina looked excited.

"Of course. Yes, he's a serious climber and his collection in his private library was superb. Alright, I'll bring them in and price them. But some of them will be very costly."

"I don't think money is a problem with him." Nora smiled.

"If you sell them to him, Nora, your bonus at the end of the week will be substantial." Georgina added, passing books to Troy who was listening with interest.

It took about half an hour to sort through the entire van for the bargain books and carry them through to Cara who started to price them with her red pencil. Georgina and Nora then went through the mountaineering books. There were some excellent tomes. Georgina priced a first edition copy of 'Scrambles amongst the Alps in the Years 1860-69 by Edward Whymper' at three hundred pounds. It was in splendid condition with a tight, clean green cloth binding, engraved plates, folding maps and wood engravings.

There was also a very fine copy of 'Narrative of an Ascent to the Summit of Mont Blanc, on the Eighth and Ninth of August, 1827 by John Auldjo'. It had been printed in 1830 by Longman, Rees, Orme, Brown and Green and included complete hand colour lithographs as well as maps. Georgina priced it at eight hundred pounds.

In all, they put aside one whole box of specialist mountaineering books and Georgina said that if the Duke had no interest in them then she had several other trade customers who would buy them anyway. Nora thanked her and Georgina and Troy headed off to Seatown for lunch.

"They look very special." Cara admired as Nora browsed through a mountaineering tome. "His Grace will be completely besotted with you when you offer him these."

Nora grinned.

"Yes, these are very rare. How fortuitous."

"Hmm. It's meant to be. Have you told him?"

"No, I'll surprise him when he comes down." Nora said happily.

"Oh I say!" A woman called into the shop.

Nora and Cara looked up.

"A pigeon has pooped all over your postcards!" She said.

Nora and Cara stared.

"Ugh. Lovely." Nora grimaced.

Cara passed Nora a pair of latex gloves from a box of two hundred pairs kept under the counter.

"Thanks!" Nora sighed, pulled them on, grabbed some tissues and headed out.

"You can't just clean them and sell them on!" The woman looked indignant.

"It happens a lot." Nora explained. "They just need a good wipe."

"How horrid." The woman left with her nose screwed up, leaving Nora shaking her head.

"That looks like a fun job." Sam from the butcher shop said, stopping next to Nora.

She was peering up at the pigeon on the window ledge and turned away to look at Sam.

"Oh. Yes, delightful isn't it?" She smiled.

Sam grabbed her arm.

"Watch out!"

"Oh no!" Nora exclaimed and then burst out laughing as more pigeon poop descended on the cards.

Sam laughed too.

"Maybe you should change their location." He suggested.

"That sounds like a good idea." Nora looked in dismay at the white excrement oozing over several racks of postcards. "Ugh, I think I'll wheel it to join the other one on the other side of the door. There are no window ledges above that one!"

"Need a hand?"

"No, it'll keep me busy. Thanks." Nora smiled.

Sam winked and set off, leaving Nora pulling out the soiled cards. She made a small pile on the pavement, moved the blue sand pudding, wheeled the postcard spinner along to position next to the other and placed the weight there. It was blocking the path a little and covering part of the estate agents window but it seemed to be the only solution.

"Ah, the joys of selling postcards." Nora sighed sarcastically as she returned to the shop carrying the poopy cards.

"Eeeeeew! I think those ones should be thrown." Cara said.

"I agree." Nora nodded and tossed them in the bin.

She washed her hands and then helped Cara sell a load of books from the Bargain Book Yard. Half an hour later, their stomachs were starting to rumble.

"I'll go and order some cheesy chips and bring them back here to eat." Cara decided. "I don't need a lunch break. I'm enjoying doing this."

She had almost marked up all the new stock and it sat waiting to be put in the yard.

"Good idea. Order me some too and we'll eat behind the counter."

"Okay." Cara grinned, standing up and stretching.

While Cara was in the café by the newsagents, Humphrey pulled up in his truck. Nora smiled to see him walk past the window carrying four boxes at once. She always marvelled at his strength.

"Hi!" She greeted, hurrying to help him.

She took the top box to reveal his face and laughed when she saw one end of a whole Mars bar clamped between his teeth.

"Hello!" Humphrey murmured, following her through the walkway of books to behind the counter. "Shall I take these straight through?"

"Would you?" Nora asked. "Thanks, Humphrey."

"No problem." He nodded, heading off through the walkway. "I'll shove the books on any empty spaces on the shelves, too. You can always sort them out later if you want."

"Thanks!" Nora dropped the box she was carrying next to the full boxes of stock that Cara had priced up from Troy and Georgina's call.

It was so crowded with boxes and piles of books that Nora felt smothered. She fanned her hand before her face, looking around in dismay. The sooner they put all the bargain books in the yard the better. It was getting impossible to move.

Nora climbed over the boxes to reach the till as a customer held up a new Ordnance Survey map to buy, and almost broke her neck.

"Wow. The shelves have been stripped out there!" Humphrey said ten minutes later, finally returning with the empty boxes.

Cara had just arrived with two covered plates of cheesy chips and two cans of coke.

"Hey, Humphrey." She greeted.

"Hi, Cara. You've been busy selling bargain books then."

"Tons of them." Cara nodded, scrambling over the boxes to get behind the till.

She almost fell into Nora who grabbed the plates quickly.

Humphrey laughed.

"This place is bedlam." He decided. "You ladies have your lunch and I'll take this next lot through."

Nora and Cara watched in admiration as he piled up four boxes, lifted them and headed off.

"He's very strong." Cara sighed.

"Amazingly so." Nora agreed.

They sat behind the counter and wiped their hands on wet wipes before tucking into their lunches hungrily, interrupted numerous times by customers buying books, selling books or asking ludicrous questions.

"My brother Fred wrote war journals during the First World War." One lady said. "Would you have them?"

Cara looked blank.

"Where's the carpet of flowers?" One lady demanded.

"That's only here over the summer." Nora explained.

"Is there a port where I can catch a ship?" One man asked.

"Erm…no." Cara assured.

"Can I use your toilet?" A beefy man enquired.

"No, sorry." Nora refused.

"Can I bring my motorbike in while I browse?" A man clad in leather asked.

Cara choked on some chips.

"I'm afraid not." Nora refused.

A married couple brought a pile of books to the counter.

"Oh I'd like to put this shop in my pocket and take it home." The wife declared. "It's wonderful."

"Thank you." Nora smiled, wiping cheese off of her fingers to take the books.

"Have you got any glue? My heel came off my shoe in your Bargain Book Yard." She asked.

"Oh. No, nothing that strong, I'm afraid." Nora replied, running the prices of the books through the till.

"Okay. My poor husband here couldn't do your stairs. Sometimes he can't even walk because of his bunions."

The husband looked outraged.

"I do not have bunions!" He protested.

"What was it then? Oh, corns." The wife corrected.

"Not *corns!* A corn. Between my toes!" The husband said.

Nora tried not to smile as she listened to them arguing.

"These books are wonderful. What a good idea to have a Black Friday sale." The wife praised.

"Thank you." Nora nodded.

"Are you doing well?" The husband asked.

"Yes, it's been very successful." Nora replied.

"You won't be closing anytime soon then. That's good. There's a sad loss of bookshops in the world these days." The husband lamented.

"Yes, it is a shame when they close." Nora agreed.

They left happy, the wife walking a bit funny because one of her shoe heels was missing. Nora finished her cheesy chips, wiped her hands and then decided to help Humphrey in the Bargain Book Yard while Cara marked up the last of the books and had a tidy up.

"Hello." Nora smiled, amazed at the improvement in the yard.

Humphrey turned from placing books on a top shelf.

"Oh, hey. Looks much better, eh?"

"A vast improvement." Nora nodded.

She went over to the boxes and gathered an armful to put on the shelves too. She then decided to salvage the tables and do some better displays.

"I can't believe how successful it's been." Nora told Humphrey.

"I'm glad." He smiled.

"The air conditioning unit came on earlier."

Humphrey burst out laughing.

"That's bad. Did anyone get blown away?"

Nora giggled.

"No." She pondered Humphrey thoughtfully, watching him slide some books along a middle shelf to make room for new stock. "So, heard anything from Jenny?"

Humphrey held still before turning to look at Nora.

"Why?"

"Oh, just wondered." She shrugged.

His eyes narrowed.

"Trying to break up with me, are you?"

"Humphrey! I already told you we're just friends anyway."

Humphrey's jaw clenched.

"I know." He turned back and began to put the books on the shelf noisily.

Nora watched him. She then walked over and hugged him hard. Humphrey held still before turning to her and hugging her back.

"I'd like us to remain together." He sighed.

"You still love Jenny." Nora said. "I saw that at the Halloween Ball."

"Not the same way as I love you."

"Like a sister."

"Hardly!"

"You can't have two people and nor can I."

"This is the twenty first century."

"That's scandalous." Nora laughed, eased away and went back to her table display.

Humphrey watched her.

"Okay. I do still love Jenny. I was almost married to her and I would have married her if she hadn't have had to go to Canada." He admitted. "It wouldn't have mattered if I had never seen her again or if you weren't ogling the Duke but seeing as that's the case I'm prepared to face that."

"That's cool."

"Cool." Humphrey's lips twitched.

Nora smiled.

"Let's just be good friends, Humphrey."

"Alright, we'll have a trial basis. I'll go out with Jenny and see if I still have real feelings for her and you go out with his Royal Highness. You'll see he doesn't compare to me." Humphrey decided.

Nora grinned.

"Thanks, Humphrey. I think that's a good plan."

"And we'll be honest with each other. I'll let you know how things are going with Jenny. She texted and asked if we could meet up."

"Then you should." Nora said, holding a book up to her face.

Humphrey glanced at her, held still and laughed.

Nora was holding a copy of 'The Fool's Girl' by Celia Rees, which had one half of a woman's face on the cover. Nora had positioned it so that it was perfectly aligned with the opposite side of half of her face.

She grinned and laughed too, turning back to continue her display, pleased that she and Humphrey had finally come to a logical arrangement.

It took a good hour to salvage the Bargain Book Yard and make it look as beautiful as before. The new stock looked great and soon, fresh bargain hunters were eagerly rummaging and snapping up the books.

Humphrey took away the empty boxes to give them more room out the front, bade goodbye and headed off after Nora and Cara had lavished him with accolades of praise and gratitude for helping out.

At half past two, rain clouds started to gather so Cara brought in the postcard spinners and squashed them by the Cole section opposite the front door. It seemed as though a coach of tourists had arrived in Castletown and soon a crowd of people filled the shop.

Nora was serving customers postcards, books and bargains when she noticed a man browsing through a book by the Folio Society section. He wore a black baseball cap, green and black check shirt and over it a hiking or hunting vest with pockets and zips, paired with jeans and boots. When he glanced at her she grinned to see that it was the Duke of Cole.

The Duke waited until Nora had served the last of her customers and put back the book.

"You weren't wrong about being busy, Nora." He smiled, stopping in front of the counter.

Cara stared, delighted.

"It really has been, Your Grace." She nodded.

He nodded hello to Cara who stood up from the swivel chair and gave him a respectful curtsey.

"Good afternoon, Your Grace." She gazed.

"Hello again, Cara."

Cara was thrilled and impressed he had remembered her name. She moved away to tidy up the mounds of books before the window, watching her sister-in-law and the Duke while fantasising what it would be like to have the Duke of Cole as her brother-in-law.

"Ah, imagine that." She muttered to herself dreamily.

"Book one." Nora smiled, passing the Duke his copy of 'The Missing Candlesticks."

"This looks excellent." He grinned, examining the book.

"How are you getting on with 'Very good, Jeeves'?"

"Very good." He smiled.

They chatted about the story and the Duke then shared the events of his day at the castle, amusing Nora with eccentric and fascinating stories.

"I have a surprise for you." Nora finally said.

The Duke looked interested.

He watched her turn towards a large box which she picked up. Suddenly the Duke was besides her, helping.

"That looks heavy." He said.

"Oh, I have bookshop muscles." Nora assured, aware of him now very close to her.

They looked at one another until they heard a small squeak.

Cara was staring at them wistfully. Nora cleared her throat and indicated towards the stool. She and the Duke placed the box on top and he watched her pick up one of the books from inside.

"Georgina acquired these today and I thought of you." Nora explained.

The Duke looked from Nora down to the book she held. He stared at it.

"Wow." He said and took it from her at Nora's urging. He read the title, obviously familiar with it. "This is rare."

"Ah, that one has been signed by members of the 1953 Everest team. George Lowe, George Band, Michael Ward and Mike Westmacott." Nora explained.

The Duke looked up to gaze at her.

"Knew it." Cara smirked to herself, seeing the Duke's expression.

He opened the copy of 'I'll climb Everest alone. The Story of Maurice Wilson by Dennis Roberts'. It had a pristine dust wrapper.

"They're very specialist so a little costly." Nora explained, pointing to the pencilled price of two hundred pounds.

The Duke didn't even flinch.

"This is a beautiful copy. I have a copy at home but nowhere near as fine as this." He breathed reverently. "I'd like to purchase this, Nora. And any more from this box that we can discover."

Nora smiled.

"I'm glad you like them, Your Grace."

"Please. Call me James." He asked her quietly, meeting her eyes before examining the book again.

Nora watched him, breathlessly.

"Alright. James."

He smiled at her and then noticed a customer.

"Can I help, sir?" Cara asked loudly, lunging for the counter.

Nora smirked as Cara gestured for Nora and the Duke to move back towards the small corridor that led to under the stairs behind the counter. James hoisted up the box and Nora the stool and they moved out of the way to explore the books.

For the next hour, Nora and the Duke of Cole devoured the collection of mountaineering books, looking at maps, plates and signatures, making a careful pile that James wished to purchase. Nora and Cara listened to his tales of climbing and expeditions and he in turn listened to their knowledge of the printing history and condition of the specialist volumes. Cara made them a round of tea and served the many customers, none of whom recognised the Duke of Cole behind the counter.

Finally, James nodded for Nora to run the prices through the till. As she did so he took out his wallet.

"I think you're going to guarantee us a healthy bonus today." Nora said as she put the large figures into the till.

James grinned, passing each one to her.

The total figure came to just under six thousand pounds. Nora stared as James passed her his card.

"Wowzers." Cara breathed, watching Nora type the total carefully into the PDQ machine. It was the largest single sale they had ever taken.

James put in his pin number, amused at their excitement.

When the sale was complete, Nora carefully wrapped each book in paper, watched by an admiring James, and then placed them gently into several cotton bags. James texted Jeeves to come to The Secondhand Bookworm to help him carry the books home to the castle and while they waited, Nora gave him a tour of the Bargain Book Yard.

"Excuse me! Can you read this to me please? The writing's so small in this book and I've forgotten my glasses." A small man asked the Duke.

"Allow me, sir." Nora smirked, taking the book and reading him the back blurb.

James watched, amused and impressed as Nora dealt with the customer, followed by two more people asking crazy questions such as:

"Any cheap books about scalp remedies?"

"I'm looking for multiple copies of this in Japanese. Would you have some?"

"I think I might like to work here." James mused, pondering the Bargain Book Yard as the customers left.

"You wouldn't." Nora assured with a laugh.

"I would. I like the company. Very much." He said.

Nora looked at him beside her.

When she saw him staring at her meaningfully, her mouth went dry.

"They can be very smelly." She said faintly.

His shoulders shook with laughter.

"I'm not referring to the customers." He pointed out.

"Oh." Nora squeaked.

They stood facing each other in the middle of the Bargain Book Yard. Nora was faintly aware of the sound of rain, pattering gently on the plastic roof above them. She began to think of magical worlds and romance stories. For a long moment they stood, looking at one another, until the sound of a polite clearing of a man's throat drew their attention.

James and Nora looked towards the doorway to see Jeeves.

"Jeeves." James smiled.

"Your Grace." Jeeves nodded. "Miss Jolly." He smiled.

"Hello, Jeeves." Nora smiled back.

They headed back to the front of The Secondhand Bookworm where Cara was serving customers. She had brought in the cheap paperback boxes, the bargain trolley and the box of free maps from outside when the rain had started. When she saw Nora and the Duke she smiled.

"Thank you for a wonderful afternoon, Nora." James told her quietly as they gathered up his bags, passing them to Jeeves.

"Thank you." She returned warmly. "I'm pleased you were able to add to your collection of mountaineering books."

"As am I. I shall start 'The Missing Candlesticks' tonight."

"I think you'll enjoy it."

"I'm sure I shall."

He gave her a lingering look before taking his leave, thanking Cara, bidding her goodbye and setting off with Jeeves who produced an umbrella for the Duke on the doorstep. Nora and Cara watched as the Duke gave one last warm salute to Nora before heading off up the hill towards his private castle entrance.

Once he had gone, Nora and Cara looked at one another.

"Oh...my...gosh." Cara breathed and covered her mouth with a squeal.

"Shhhhh!" Nora laughed.

"He is adorable." Cara sighed, dreamily. "And I can't believe he bought all those books. Well, actually I can. You found them for him and he simply couldn't resist."

Nora laughed, staring at the figure written in the cash book, her head spinning.

"Well, that was a truly incredible end to Black Friday at The Secondhand Bookworm." Nora decided, amazed.

"It really was. Please let me tell Seymour?" She begged.

"Go on then." Nora laughed. "And we must let Georgina know how much the Duke of Cole spent!"

"James." Cara corrected with a grin.

"James." Nora agreed, grinning too.

"And let's tell Roger too. It'll drive him mad!"

Laughing, Nora agreed.

At five o'clock, Cara and Nora closed down the computer and shrugged into their coats, pleased and worn out after a mammoth Black Friday trading. Nora was yawning behind her hands as they set the alarm, turned off the lights and locked up The Secondhand Bookworm for the night.

Cara noticed Seymour's van parked across the road and gave a wave. She and Nora headed over under Nora's big cream umbrella to fuss over Arthur who was excited to see Cara.

"Congratulations." Seymour said and winked at his sister.

"Thanks. It was a great day." Nora smiled.

"So I heard." He winked again, meaningfully.

Nora gave him a look.

"I'm starving!" Cara exclaimed, climbing into the cab and kissing her husband.

"Want to join us for dinner, sis?" Seymour asked.

Nora shook her head.

"Thanks but I'm in need of a long soak in the bath after that day." She declined.

"Speak to you tomorrow!" Cara grinned.

Nora nodded and closed the truck door for her.

Seymour beeped the horn and they waved goodbye and once they were on their way Nora crossed back to her side of the road, setting off up the hill with her thoughts full of bargain books, mountains, Book Clubs and, most importantly, *James*.

11 THE CASE OF THE MISSING BIFFA BIN

Heather Jolly arrived at The Secondhand Bookworm fresh and raring to go on what she had Christened 'Serious Selling Saturday'. Her sister Nora was yawning behind a book and her cousin, Felix, was emptying the waste paper bin into a black sack as Heather strolled cheerfully in.

"Ready for some 'Serious Selling Saturday' fun?" She asked with a grin.

"The fun's already begun." Nora jerked her thumb behind her in the direction of the back of the shop where loud noises could be heard.

"What's that?" Heather asked curiously.

"Hatchet-Face and Pig-Goat are salvaging a bookcase and part of a wall after drilling through too far yesterday evening." Felix explained.

Heather giggled at the terrible nicknames.

"I take it those are the mad people next door."

"Hmm." Nora nodded, biting into an apple. "I said they've got until ten to finish up. Pig-Goat is mending one of the bookcases. When I looked into the Bargain

Book Yard this morning, the case was face down on the floor where his drill bit had forced it over. He came around and apologised and begged me not to tell Georgina. They've almost salvaged it."

"I love working here." Heather smiled happily.

Felix gave her a look.

"Must have been a racket if they were drilling all evening."

"Glad I live up the hill and far away." Nora nodded.

"Are you going to tell Georgina?"

"No. Pig-Goat looked really scared."

They all laughed.

Nora told Heather to pop her bag and coat under the stairs, watching her sister stare in amazement at the mountains of books everywhere. Everything that went outside had already been placed on the pavement or clipped against the wall by Nora and Felix who had both arrived early. The autumn farmer's market had been trading since eight o'clock and Hugh was organising cones and barriers to close the high street roads ready for the sheep racing at noon.

People were already arriving for the bargain books.

"Good morning." A man eating a huge pumpkin pasty greeted.

"Erm…" Nora grimaced at his food but since she was eating an apple herself she felt she couldn't tell him off for coming into the bookshop with it.

"Hello, sir." Felix replied politely.

"Your Bargain Book Yard? Is it still open?"

"Yes, sir. And everything must go today!" Felix enthused.

"Grand, grand." The man took an enormous bite of his pasty so they all saw his tonsils.

"Through the back there." Heather instructed, trying not to retch as he chewed loudly with his mouth open.

"Thank you!" He said, spraying pastry everywhere.

Nora reached for her umbrella.

Once he had disappeared into the back, Heather brushed some wet flakes from her blue The Secondhand Bookworm t-shirt.

"What's the plan for today?" She asked Nora.

"Sell, sell, sell!" Nora replied.

"May I go and check on the Bargain Book Yard?"

"Please do. Our mission will be to keep it tidy and saleable."

Hatchet-Face moped through.

"We're done." She said flatly and left carrying a saw.

Nora, Felix and Heather stared.

"Old hatchet face." Felix muttered, hoisting up the black sack. "I'll take this to the Biffa bin now."

"Thanks, Felix." Nora appreciated.

He followed Hatchet-Face with the black sack over his shoulder like Father Christmas, pausing to let a stream of people through the doorway into the shop. Heather snuck off to examine the Bargain Book Yard where Pig-Goat was sweeping away the mess he had made and speaking to Pumpkin-Pasty man. She reported back to Nora that everything looked lovely in the yard and was very enticing.

"Hopefully we'll sell the lot today." Nora smiled.

"So we'll keep this hush-hush then." Pig-Goat said as he came into the front of the shop with his tool box.

"No problem." Nora promised.

He smiled.

"Thank you, Nora. Sorry once again for the mishap. We've almost finished our renovations."

"Great." She nodded.

He bade goodbye and headed off. Nora smirked.

"Bargain Book Yard?" A woman demanded, arriving with loads of noisy children.

"Right at the back through the kitchen." Nora pointed.

"Where are your cheap books?" An old man asked. He had a very red nose and runny eyes.

"Eeewww…I mean, through there and in the back." Nora gestured.

A family arrived looking like Hillbillies.

"Books." The elder said, chewing a straw.

"Cheapuns please." His wife added.

There were wood shavings in her hair.

The children were screaming.

"Right at the back." Nora shouted.

They headed off, meeting a traffic jam in the walkway. The children started to push and kick and an old man swore loudly.

"Oh dear. This is going to be a fun day." Nora sighed.

Heather couldn't see because she was laughing so much.

More people arrived, trailed by Felix who was still carrying the black sack of rubbish. He looked stressed.

"I can't find the Biffa bin anywhere!" He whined loudly.

"What?" "Nora looked bemused.

"Isn't it where it always is?" Heather asked.

Felix gave her a look.

"I do have eyes. I've hunted everywhere."

"Oh dear." Nora sighed.

"Maybe it's been moved." Heather proposed.

"Why don't you both go hunting for it? Check around the back of the restaurants and snoop around the town."

"On it!" Heather grabbed her coat and pushed Felix out of the door again with his sack while he protested and assured her he had looked everywhere.

A Skype message arrived so Nora leaned forward to read it.

'Dead here! Xxx' Cara had written.

'Insane here. And someone has stolen our Biffa bin xxx' Nora replied.

'Whaaaaaat?! Hope you find it! X'

Nora smirked, turning to the counter as people arrived to pay for their books.

One man wearing an eyepatch and carrying a large pumpkin spent fifty pounds on books from the Bargain Book Yard. Three more people bought loads of cheap books and moaned about the prices on the rest of the shop shelves. Nora glowered.

There was a constant queue, knocking over the mountains of books that appeared to release fleas. Several people stood scratching their arms and legs while waiting. Nora was sure she could see fleas leaping about the cash book.

"Gross." She said, flopping into the chair once everyone had gone.

Heather and Felix returned with the bag of rubbish.

"No luck anywhere." Heather said. "But I bought us some hot boar sausage rolls from the autumn farmer's market."

"Oh yum." Nora sat up eagerly.

"I'm at a loss." Felix said, leaving the black sack by the door. "Confused emoji."

"I suppose we should report it missing." Nora mused. She bit into her sausage roll.

"Yes, we should report it as a crime." Felix agreed.

"Phone 101." Nora suggested through her mouthful.

Felix marched over to the counter and picked up the telephone receiver.

"I will. I won't have people stealing our property." He glowered and dialled the number.

Nora and Heather watched and listened with interest, eating their sausage rolls.

"Hello. I'd like to report a crime." Felix said firmly. "My name and problem? My name is Felix Jolly and I'm here to report a missing bin."

There was a long silence.

"Oh, erm…I think it went missing overnight."

Nora and Heather fought hard not to giggle.

"Well, I've looked in the moat." Felix told the woman on the end of the phone.

Heather choked on her sausage roll.

After giving her the location details of The Secondhand Bookworm he concluded:

"Thirty days? Okay, thank you. Yes, I'll let you know if it turns up." Felix said and ended the call. "Well I've reported it." He said, staring at his cousins who were both laughing.

"I'm sorry, Felix." Nora apologised, wiping her eyes. "It was when you said you had looked in the moat…"

Felix's lips twitched.

"Is it alright if we come in?" A loud voice called from the doorway. "We're coming in!"

Nora, Heather and Felix stared as two very large people struggled in the doorway together, fighting to enter The Secondhand Bookworm.

"Do you have a copy of 'The Astonishing Adventures of Mr Weems and the She Vampires'?" The large man asked.

Felix scoffed.

"Er…no. That's a retro computer game, not a book." He said bluntly.

The man looked offended.

"I know my computer games." Felix assured. "Even ones from the eighties and nineties. I'm a serious gamer."

"He is." Nora agreed.

"Well I thought it was a book. My son was telling me about it at our Halloween party. Forget it then." The large man huffed.

"We have a brilliant Bargain Book Yard out the back." Heather chirped in.

The man paused.

"Oh let's go and have a look, Barney." The woman with him said.

"Alright then. Which way?" Barney demanded.

"Through there, through the kitchen and you can't miss it. Fifty percent off the marked prices inside." Nora explained.

They hurried really quickly and almost got wedged in the walkway.

Felix sniggered.

"Should I tell Georgina about the missing Biffa bin?" He then asked.

"I would. She likes to be kept appraised of things like that." Nora nodded.

Felix picked up the phone and squashed himself in the walkway under the stairs as suddenly customers bearing bargain books and books from about the shop surrounded them like zombies. Nora and Heather spent five minutes dealing with them until Felix finished speaking with Georgina and helped. They set up a conveyer belt system where Felix took the customer's books and read out the prices to Nora who punched the prices in the till and passed them to Heather who bagged them up. It worked really well and only two people had a tantrum about being forcibly given bags.

"What did Georgina say about the Biffa bin?" Nora asked Felix as they wiped their hands on wet wipes and Felix devoured his cold sausage roll.

"Oh she said 'typical' and moaned for five whole minutes in my ear. At one point I think she was implying that I had stolen it. I sarcastically agreed that I collected Biffa bins."

Nora burst out laughing.

"Look!" Heather exclaimed. "The Tiny Tim van has arrived!"

Nora and Felix flew across the room, trying not to get too close to the flea-books, and watched as a brightly coloured van reversed onto the cobbles where a donkey-pen had been erected.

"Awwwww." They all cooed as a farmer led Tiny Tim down a ramp and into the pen.

Tiny Tim promptly went to the toilet before turning his back on everyone to eat. Felix found that really funny and spent the next ten minutes laughing and sniggering about it behind the counter, until Nora sent him off to buy three La Limonatas from the delicatessen.

Heather and Felix were serving customers as midday approached while Nora was sifting through the flea books and taking armfuls upstairs. She had had a quick look around the shop and had been astonished at the gaps in the shelves in all sections, so decided to try and make some more room in the front because of the amount of people.

So far, Nora had managed to carry eight piles up and place them quickly onto the shelves in their sections. Unfortunately it didn't look much different in the front room.

Nora was happily pulling out any books about needlework from the piles when she noticed the bargain book trolley wheeling away past the window.

"What the…" In a few seconds she had leaped out of the shop to see a child merrily pushing it up the street.

"Stop!" Nora called.

A woman dove after her son.

"I'm so sorry. Is it yours?" She apologised, grabbing the boy by the nose.

Nora stared.

"Erm…" She was too distracted by the boy who had become motionless as his mother held his nose firmly.

"I've told you before, Kenny, not to help yourself to objects!" The mother scolded him.

"No problem…it goes in front of our bookshop."
Nora said, taking hold of the trolley and rolling it back,
glancing at the mother who still had the boy's nose in
between her finger and thumb.

"You shouldn't have so much stuff on the pavement."
A familiar voice said.

Nora knew it was Hugh.

"Can if I like." She retorted.

He was staring at her but smirked slightly.

"Your funeral. If some old codger trips and gets his
head run over in the road it's your fault." Hugh said.

Nora decided to change the subject.

"Have you seen our Biffa bin?"

He looked at her stupidly.

"Why?"

"Because it has gone missing." Nora said.

Hugh's eyes widened.

"What? You're flippin' joking?!"

"No, I'm not. In fact my colleague has just reported it
to Crimewatch UK."

Hugh's eyes bulged.

"I'll go and have a look myself." He decided.

"Thank you." Nora smiled sweetly and sighed as he
stalked off.

"Your Biffa bin was stolen?"

Nora turned towards the owner of the familiar voice
and her stomach turned several pleasant loops.

"Oh. James." She said, surprised.

The Duke of Cole smiled broadly at her use of his
first name.

"Hello, Nora."

They stared at one another for a long moment. He
was 'in disguise' again, wearing casual, good quality
outdoor clothes and a baseball cap, this time with added
black rimmed glasses. No one recognised him except, of
course, Nora.

"Yes, our Biffa bin has gone missing. Are you here to do some shopping?"

"I'm sorry to hear that. No. I'm here to see you." James smiled.

"Oh." Nora grinned.

"How are you?"

"Okay. You?"

"Very well." The Duke continued to smile.

They remained on the pavement outside The Secondhand Bookworm until Nora invited James inside.

"Would you like a cup of tea?"

The Duke was watching Nora intently.

"I'd love one. Do you have a lunch break soon?"

Nora checked her watch.

"I can do, yes." She nodded.

Heather and Felix were staring as Nora returned in the company of the Duke of Cole. They both recognised him and stood with their mouths slightly open.

"Hello." James greeted.

"Your…your Grace." Heather curtsied.

Felix continued to stare.

"I sent Hugh off to do some bin investigating." Nora told her sister and cousin. "Would you like tea? I'll put the kettle on."

"Yes please." Heather and Felix chorused, bemused.

"We'll be in the kitchen." Nora said, winked at them and led James off.

"It seems busy here today." James observed as they squashed into the tiny kitchen. He peered into the Bargain Book Yard, fascinated to see the people fighting over bargains.

"People are here for the autumn farmer's market. There's a sheep race at noon."

James chuckled.

"I heard about that."

"I'd like to see it." Nora smirked.

"I'll join you"."

Nora gave him a warm look.

"It's nice to see you in town. How are things up at the castle?"

He shrugged.

"To be honest, all I could think about was you working in The Secondhand Bookworm today." He said, opening a cupboard and passing her four mugs.

"Really?" Nora squeaked.

He grinned.

"Yes."

Nora filled up the kettle with water, feeling herself blush. She cleared her throat.

"How are your mountaineering books?"

"Very fine." James praised.

Somehow he managed to find the caddy of tea bags so added one each to the mugs. Nora admired his domesticity. As they waited for the water to boil, James leaned against the worktop, arms folded, chatting easily about his library and asking if Nora would like to help him organise his mountaineering section.

"It would be my honour!" She exclaimed, pleased.

"Are you free tonight?" He hoped.

Nora smiled but shook her head.

"I have plans."

James frowned.

"Humphrey?" He looked disappointed.

"No." Nora assured. She opened the fridge for the milk. "Humphrey and I finally had a talk yesterday and agreed to see other people."

When she looked back at the Duke he was smiling broadly.

"I'm glad."

"The plans that I have are with my sister. Heather bought a retro games console in the lead up to Black Friday, one we used to play with our brothers when we

191

were children. It's a Jupiter Cube Console with six games. I know it's silly, but we thought we'd take a trip down memory lane."

The Duke of Cole looked amazed.

"I remember the Jupiter Cube." He admitted.

"You do?" Nora smiled.

"It was very rare. My father helped to design several consoles when he patronized specific computing companies back in the eighties so I learned a lot about them as a boy. He worked on the Jupiter Cube."

"That's very clever." Nora was impressed.

"The only console I ever actually played when I was a boy happened to be the Jupiter Cube."

"That's the only one I ever played too."

They regarded one another with deeper interest. Nora found herself imagining a young Duke boy playing Wizzingball all alone on a 1980's game console in a magnificent castle. The Duke imagined a young girl sitting watching her brothers and being allowed to have a go.

"Would you like to play on ours?" She invited.

"Yes!" The Duke answered fervently.

Nora laughed and he grinned.

"But I won't impose upon you and your sister."

"It would be no imposition. I know for a fact that Heather would love to play Triple Dragon with the Duke of Cole." Nora assured.

James grinned, accepting with a small incline of his head.

They finished making the tea and carried the mugs through to the front of the shop which was teeming with people. Before Nora could tell Heather that they would be playing retro computer games with the Duke of Cole, Hugh loomed up to the doorway.

"I found your bin!" He hollered loudly.

A woman dropped her bag of parsnips in alarm.

Nora, Heather, Felix and the Duke of Cole all stared at him from behind the counter.

"Did you?!" Nora was amazed.

"Where was it?" Felix demanded, stunned.

"I reckon his royal highness should insist on better lighting and security cameras about the town. A group of local yobs wheeled it all the way to The Black Hart pub over the bridge." Hugh said.

Nora, Heather and Felix looked at the Duke awkwardly because of Hugh's comments. James gave a look that said he agreed and sipped his tea with an amused smile.

Nora bit back a grin.

"Thank you, Hugh." Nora appreciated.

"Well you can wheel the damned thing back." He said rudely.

James held still and Felix sniggered. Heather's eyes widened.

"No problem. Thanks for finding it." Nora humoured.

"It's in their beer garden. I said you would be over to collect it. OY! That git!" Hugh then shouted at some litterer in the street and stomped off.

The Duke's shoulders were shaking with silent laughter.

"Excuse me, handsome fellow." An old woman addressed the Duke, waving a book in his face. "This is priced too high."

James took it with a smile.

Smirking, Nora took the book from the Duke of Cole and passed it to Felix who was sniggering into his mug.

"Why don't we go and rescue the Biffa bin?" Nora suggested, tugging lightly on the Duke's sleeve and gesturing toward the door.

She felt him take her hand.

"Please let's do." He nodded, enjoying himself.

Nora glanced down at their hands joined and then glanced back at Heather as she and the Duke of Cole left.

Heather was grinning broadly and stuck up her thumb, watching them go. Her head dizzy with amusement and happiness, Nora left The Secondhand Bookworm to go and rescue a Biffa bin from a beer garden with the Duke of Cole!

'Serious Selling Saturday' was certainly living up to its name. When Nora and James returned after having put the Biffa bin back in its rightful home, stopping to examine some wild flowers growing by the ancient town walls and read some historical signs, Heather and Felix were having a great time dealing with crowds of people.

James and Nora helped out and the bookworm staff were amused that nobody was aware that the Duke of Cole was bagging up their books and wishing them a good day. At quarter to midday the traffic stopped and a rare silence fell upon the town. Everyone went outside to watch the sheep race so Nora, James, Felix and Heather crowded outside The Secondhand Bookworm door.

Alice and Philip from the delicatessen seemed to be suspicious of the tall, handsome man standing with Nora and kept looking over to the bookshop group and then conferring with one another. In the end, Alice sent her son Grey over just as the sheep were herded to the top of the hill.

"Hello, Grey." Nora smiled, bemused.

"Hello. Mum wants to know who your friend is."

"James." The Duke said with a charming smile.

Grey peered at him curiously so Nora waved over to Alice and winked.

Grey headed back to the delicatessen group and told Alice the Duke's name. Alice's eyes widened and she pretended to lock her lips and throw away the key, giving Nora an impressed look.

The sheep race began with lots of cheering and baaing. It was hilarious and Nora and James doubled over laughing as the sheep tore down the steep road, leaping majestically over bales of hay with their teddy bear jockeys on their backs.

Nora could hear Leo, the Goat-Lady's charcoal burning son, commentating on the race through a megaphone which finally ended with him calling out: "Betty the Badger Face Welsh Mountain wins by a head, beating Maggie the British Milksheep who gets second place!"

Everyone cheered and the sheep were fussed over, fed and returned to their trucks.

Back in the shop, Heather and Felix told Nora to take her lunch break with the Duke as it would probably be quiet for a while. Nora smiled gratefully, grabbed her bag and set off excitedly.

"I have only eaten in The Duke's Pie." James admitted, walking with Nora up the road as the bales of hay were removed, the roads swept and the traffic began to flow once more.

"There are a lot of nice cafes and restaurants here." Nora smiled.

"Anywhere quaint and quiet?"

"The Flowery Teacup has some nice solitary corners." Nora recalled.

"I like the sound of that." James nodded. "Lead the way."

"Certainly, Your Grace." Nora grinned as he took hold of her hand once more and they crossed the road.

12 GHOST WRITER

After lunch, Felix and Heather hurried off to grab sandwiches leaving Nora and the Duke of Cole serving customers behind the till. Nora was amused at how much James seemed to be enjoying himself. They had had a lovely lunch in a quiet corner of The Flowery Teacup down Market Street where no one recognised James, and now they stood discussing 'Triple Dragon' game strategies in between serving customers.

"Heather always says she prefers to watch. She used to sit and watch our brothers rather than play, so she will be delighted to let us have a few games tonight." Nora assured.

She couldn't help but marvel that the enigmatic Duke of Cole was keen to spend the evening at her flat playing retro video games.

"Thank you, Nora. I am an only child so I had a rather solitary childhood." The Duke shared. "One of the highlights of my childhood was playing the Jupiter Cube down in the kitchens of James Hall with Jeeves. We often played 'Triple Dragon'."

"How lovely." Nora said, thinking how kind that was of Jeeves. Nora had read what little information there was about the Duke of Cole who was renowned for being both solitary and brave. "I read about your mountain climbing achievements. You prefer to do solo climbing, without a belay?" She worried.

"Free solo climbing." The Duke nodded. "But I don't do that anymore."

"That's good." Nora looked relieved.

The Duke smiled, pleased at her concern.

"Excuse me! Yes, you there. Love birds." A man interrupted rudely.

Nora and James looked at him. Nora's eyes popped but James grinned.

"Do you have a copy of 'The Great Gatsby'? In cheap paperback." The man asked.

"Have you looked in the Bargain Book Yard?" James asked.

"Of course I have, sonny!" The man exclaimed.

Nora was worried about her customers being disrespectful to the Duke of Cole but James seemed to be enjoying it.

"We could possibly have a copy in the attic room." Nora said hastily.

"Oh. I don't do stairs!"

"I can have a look for you." James offered.

Nora was amazed.

"Oh. Would you? Thank you young man." The customer nodded stiffly.

"Alphabetical order of author?" James asked Nora with a smile.

"Yes. Are you sure?"

"Of course." He smiled and set off.

"Are you engaged?" The customer asked Nora before James was out of earshot.

Before she could reply she saw James lean back around the rare bookcase.

"There's an idea." He mouthed, grinned and continued on his way upstairs.

Nora felt her heart do a triple leap. She just stared at the customer mutely.

"Is Felix here?" A man then demanded.

Nora jumped.

"There's a queue here!" The first customer snapped.

"I'm not here to buy books. Felix is my ghost writer." The man defended with a snarl.

Nora stared.

"Pardon?" She asked.

"Felix Jolly? Is he in today?"

Nora nodded.

"He's my ghost writer. Is he about then?"

"He's at lunch at the moment." Nora said faintly.

"Hmm. Alright, I'll come back in half an hour." The man said and stomped off leaving Nora bewildered.

Her first customer stared at her.

"What's wrong with you?" He asked.

Nora just blinked.

Fortunately several other customers arrived wishing to purchase books so Nora was distracted with the sales. James returned carrying a copy of 'The Great Gatsby'. He stood with the customer and they flicked through it. Nora was distracted as she listened to their conversation and smirked when the customer asked if James was a movie actor.

"Oh, you seem familiar. You have one of those faces." The man shrugged, taking the paperback to the counter to pay.

Felix returned with Heather.

"Felix! Someone was here asking for their ghost writer." Nora told him.

Felix did a double take.

"Which one?"

"He didn't say his name but...*ghost writer*?"

Felix smirked.

"Oh yes. A job I have on the side."

"Sorry, Your Grace." Heather apologised in a low voice as she squeezed past him behind the counter.

"I apologise. I'm in the way."

"Not at all!" Heather assured dreamily.

"I should go." He smiled and walked around to the front of the counter as The Great Gatsby customer left. "Thank you for lunch and for your company." He told Nora warmly.

"The pleasure was mine." Nora replied.

He pulled his baseball cap down a little further.

"Your place at seven?" He asked.

"Looking forward to it." Nora squeaked.

He grinned, bade Felix and Heather goodbye and left with a final glance back.

"Is the Duke coming around tonight?" Heather asked eagerly.

"Yes, I hope that's alright."

"That's more than alright!" Heather gushed. "Did you tell him we were playing retro computer games on our new Jupiter Cube?"

"He would like to join in." Nora beamed.

"I'm speechless." Heather said, amazed at having spent the morning with the Duke of Cole who would now be playing games with them that evening.

"Me too." Felix piped in.

"I'm more interested in your ghost writing!" Nora told Felix.

He jumped into the swivel chair.

"A-ha-ha. Why?" He smirked,

"Since when did you become a ghost writer?" Nora demanded.

"I was talking with a customer a few weeks back and he was telling me how he wanted to write his biography but was useless with computers. So I said I would be happy to type it out for him and edit it as he dictates. It's about his life as a transgender milkman."

Nora and Heather stared.

"Pardon?" Nora gawped.

"It's actually fascinating stuff." Felix assured with a small smirk.

"And who else do you write for?" Heather asked.

"Three others. They all pay me twenty pounds an hour. Was it a man who asked for me?"

"Yes."

"Large and hairy?"

Nora nodded.

"That's Ian. He's writing a book about capitalism. I'm going there tonight but he doesn't have a phone so he's probably come to ask me to change the day." Felix explained.

"Who are the others?" Heather asked curiously.

"A woman who's writing about her time in the Yorkshire Dales and an old lady who's writing about investment finance."

Nora didn't know what to think.

"Impressive." Heather admired, chuckling.

"Thanks." Felix appreciated. "I do about five hours a week ghost writing so it's an extra four hundred pounds a month to my wages here. I'm saving for a flat."

"Wow. Well done, Felix." Heather praised.

"That *is* impressive." Nora agreed.

"Perhaps I can rent your flat when you marry His Grace, cousin Nora?" Felix added with a small smile.

"I've got dibs on that." Heather said quickly.

Nora gave them both a look.

A woman with pink hair arrived and asked for directions to The Honey Show. Felix looked it up on the

Castletown website and said that it was taking place in the town hall along with a chutney and jam making competition, woodturning demonstrations and a cider fayre.

The farmer's autumn market stalls were being packed away with lots of banging and crashing of metal rods and poles for an afternoon of falconry displays and the Autumn Square Dancing and Folk Festival.

Ladies started to arrive at The Secondhand Bookworm in vintage check square dancing dresses with volumes of petticoats making them look like cheerleaders. They asked for books about hand bell ringing, crime novels, women's health, and dress making and several of them danced up the stairs.

A band set up on the cobbles and started to play fiddles, a banjo, a jolly accordion, guitars, a keyboard, and percussion instruments. Heather ran to the window clapping her hands in time to the music. Soon, the whole town was full of country dance music and square dancing. The man who had the falconry display looked annoyed.

Ian returned.

"Ah, Felix." He noticed, relieved.

"Hello, Ian." Felix replied, speaking very posh.

Nora and Heather looked at one another.

"I came in early and asked one of your employees where you were." Ian explained.

Felix gave his cousins a quick glance.

"I was taking a lunch break." He said, speaking as though he had a plum in his mouth.

"And so you should. Your shop is doing well?" Ian asked, looking around.

"It is thank you. I am very pleased." Felix nodded. "And I have learned a lot from your book on capitalism so far that has proven very helpful in my business."

Heather was doing her best not to dissolve into giggles.

Ian gave Nora and Heather a disdainful look.

"I'm pleased." Ian said. "Would we be able to postpone writing tonight until next week? I'll still pay you of course, as per our arrangement, but I have to go and visit my mother."

"Of course, Ian. That would be fine." Felix agreed pompously.

Nora and Heather watched Ian give Felix a twenty pound note which Felix swiped and placed into his wallet.

"See you next week." Ian said, turned and left.

When he had gone, Nora and Heather stared at Felix. He grinned.

"I tell them that I own the shop. It gives me more credibility."

"Felix!" Nora half laughed.

He shrugged and turned to read the Skype messages, one of which just read:

'HILLLLLLLLLLLLLLLLL!!!'

Nora took that to mean that Mr Hill had arrived in Seatown and she didn't envy them that!

At about three o'clock, Nora decided to tidy up the Bargain Book Yard. It was a huge mess with numerous people still rummaging. First she tidied up the tables and picked some larger books from the bookcases to display them nicely.

"Oooh, what's that? Tigers. I love tigers. How much?" One lady asked, snatching a book from Nora's hand as she stood it on the table top.

"The price is inside in red pencil."

"Ten pounds. Oh, that's too much." The woman read.

"It will be five pounds because today we are giving fifty percent off." Nora explained.

"I'll take it!" The woman almost shrieked. "Any more bargains?"

"All of these books will be half priced." Nora smirked.

"Oh my!" She proceeded to hurry around the yard, elbowing people aside and picking out numerous volumes.

One of the pumpkin face lights was flickering so Nora assumed that the batteries were reaching the end of their service. She managed to place all the books from the floor onto the shelves and turned numerous tomes to face outwards, displaying the ones with the brightest, eye-catching covers.

She then stood encouraging people to buy, showing them to sections, helping them to find books of interest and sending a steady stream of buyers back through the shop to Heather and Felix.

In the front room, the till was beeping and clunking and Felix was hastily squirreling away wads of notes so that if they were robbed most of the cash was out of the till and in the locked cash box in a secure location.

Nora remained in the yard, enjoying the pleasant atmosphere and trying not to get too attached to it because it was going to be dismantled the following week. Her bottom lip trembled because it really was a lovely room, but then she saw the outside loo and wondered if anyone else had used it, so sobered quickly.

After a while, Nora sat on the long step that elevated part of the floor by the Indian restaurant and read through a pile of books, which made people ask her where she had found each tome so she charitably handed them over and smiled as they ran off to purchase them.

She tried out many other selling tactics including walking around and exclaiming with delight at the bargain prices and the titles until one boy pointed to her blouse with the words 'The Secondhand Bookworm' embroidered on the breast that revealed she obviously worked there. Nora just smiled and continued to tidy up.

"You've been out here ages." Heather's voice floated into the yard.

"Oh yes, I'm drumming up business." Nora grinned.

"It's working. We've taken over three thousand pounds so far."

"What?!" Nora was amazed.

"I was wondering if we could fill up the bargain trolley on the pavement. I noticed it's almost empty."

"Oh that's a good idea. Help me choose some books then." Nora agreed.

"By the way, Felix is designing business cards and flyers to offer his services as a ghost writer." Heather revealed.

Nora laughed.

"He is very enterprising."

"He is!" Heather agreed.

They spent five minutes choosing books and then carried them through to the front where Felix was negotiating the sale of a large run of leather books with a trade customer.

"…and if you ever think of writing a book I would be happy to be your ghost writer." Felix was saying.

"I'll think about it." The well-dressed American nodded.

"Here is a business card." Felix offered.

Nora and Heather shook their heads as they carried the books outside to the bargain trolley.

"Oh, are they more cheap books?" The man with the eye patch who had visited The Secondhand Bookworm before asked.

"Er…yes." Nora nodded.

"Do you know a place where I can buy a shower curtain?" He enquired.

"You may need to look in Seatown." Nora replied.

"I see."

Heather gave Nora a look, obviously referring to his eye patch and his last comment. Nora bit back a giggle.

They filled up the trolley until people swarmed around and shoved them rudely out the way. Nora had to squeeze her arm between two fat people to put her last book on the top shelf of it. She and Heather then stood on the pavement watching the lively square dancing. A man passed them two maracas each.

"Join in. It's fun!" He urged.

Heather eagerly began to shake and rattle hers about in time to the music.

"Are there any haunted houses around here?" A teenage boy in a black cape asked Nora.

"Erm…well, we have a ghost under our flagstones." She replied.

The boy's dark rimmed eyes lit up.

"Really?"

"Damon! We're going to Pizza Express!" His mother shrieked.

"Just a minute. Show me." He ordered Nora.

She pointed through the doorway to the flagstones and told him the story of a boy who had died from being trapped down a well so his ghost now haunted it. Damon cheered up considerably and went off smiling oddly.

"Can you hand these out?" Felix asked, appearing on the doorstep.

He noticed Heather shaking maracas in time to the music and stared.

"What are they?" Nora asked.

"Flyers for my ghost writing services."

"No." Nora laughed.

"Sad emoji." Felix sighed and returned into the shop, leaving Nora smirking and shaking her head.

.

13 EVERYTHING MUST GO!

At four o'clock, Nora made the executive decision to offer eighty percent off on all bargain books. Felix created a large sign on the computer and printed out three copies. He stuck one in the window, one on the bargain trolley, and one at the bottom of the first staircase. They read:

ALL BOOKS MARKED IN RED PENCIL
80% OFF
IN THE BARGAIN BOOK YARD!

"Do you think it will work?" Heather asked as she ate yoghurt behind the counter.

"Yes." Nora said, pointing to a stampede of people reading the new signs and heading in.

Felix was flattened against the bookcases.

"Before we leave tonight I'd like to put my Book Club poster in the window to get some more members before it starts." Nora announced.

"Sounds good!" Felix agreed.

Nora heard a text message arrive so dug out her iPhone, smiling when she saw it was from the Duke.

'I had an amazing time with you today. Looking forward to tonight x'

"Are you two officially dating now?" Heather asked, leaning over her sister's shoulder.

Nora almost dropped the phone.

"No." She replied quickly.

"Well it looks like he seems to think so." Heather grinned.

"It's never been made official." Nora shrugged, biting back her chuffed smile as she replied to the Duke's text message.

"Are you expecting a royal declaration?"

Nora nudged her sister's elbow and Heather winked.

'I had a wonderful time too. See you soon x' She wrote.

Heather smirked.

"Eighty percent off?! All these books?" A man in a green anorak exclaimed.

"No. Just the ones in the Bargain Book Yard." Nora replied quickly.

"Where's that then?"

"I'll show you, sir. This way." Nora gestured and guided him through the shop.

"Look at all these books. Do you own them all?" He asked as they walked through the back room towards the kitchen.

"No, they're all for sale." Nora replied.

Out in the Bargain Book Yard the entire room was being ferreted. The tables were wrecked and the shelves pillaged. Nora thought Robin Hood and his Merry Men had paid a visit.

"I'd better be quick!" The man exclaimed and dove into the crowd of bargain hunters.

Nora decided to try and salvage the books again. When they were sorted and tidy they sold better and she was determined that everything would go by the end of the day.

"Do you work here?" A lady in a red bandana asked.

"Yes."

"Do you have any books about candle making out here?"

"It's possible." Nora pondered and helped her look.

"How much are the pumpkin lights?" Someone called.

"They're not for sale." Nora said.

"Can I use the loo?"

"We can't allow customers to use our staff toilet."

"That man just did."

Nora stared at a shifty looking man looking at photography books by the outside loo. She ground her teeth.

"I was taken by the square dancing on the cobbles. Do you have any books about sheep?" A man asked.

"Oh. I thought you were going to ask if we had any books about square dancing."

"Why would I do that?" He gave her an ironic look.

Nora inwardly sighed.

"Who wrote Dracula?" Someone asked.

"Bram Stoker." A woman in the crowd answered in reply.

Books were falling off of the shelves and one of the tables overturned. Nora jumped and rushed to investigate. A man had been sitting on it to read.

"This looks like bedlam." A familiar voice exclaimed.

Nora turned to see Spencer, one of her regulars, standing in the kitchen doorway.

"Oh, hello!" She smiled and nodded in agreement.

"All of these books are discounted?" He asked, gliding in with his white hair flowing gently behind him. He looked like Gandalf the White.

"Yes. Everything here must go."

"What if we buy ten? Do we get any free?" A man who looked like an elf asked.

"Yes." Nora decided. "If you purchase ten books from the Bargain Book Yard, you get two bargain books free."

There were 'ooohs' and gasps and more rummaging. Two small people who looked like Hobbits began to clear the tables. It was like a Lord of the Rings convention. Nora decided she had better inform Heather and Felix of her plan so left Spencer pursuing a shelf until all the books on it were snatched before his face.

"It's madness out there." Nora told Heather and Felix.

"It is." Spencer agreed.

Nora yelped and turned, scared that he had somehow managed to arrive so quickly from the yard. She gave him a funny look, suspecting he had used his occult powers.

"Hello." A woman said.

Nora recognised the voice at the counter and saw that it was Miss Raven.

"Oh. Hello again, Miss Raven." Nora smiled.

"Miss Raven has come to collect her book." Felix said with a pointed look at Nora. His eyebrows lowered and he gave her a secret glare. "For the Book Club."

Nora returned the glare with an apologetic look, having forgotten to inform him that Miss Raven would be joining their club.

"Any books put buy for me?" Spencer asked, suddenly standing next to Miss Raven.

"I don't believe so."

"I probably bought every esoteric book ever printed from the large amount you had for sale over Halloween." Spencer smiled, examining a Penguin book mug on the counter. "But I'll go and check out your occult section upstairs anyway."

He left, as though gliding.

Nora rummaged under the counter and took a copy of 'The Missing Candlesticks' from her Book Club box. She handed it to Miss Raven.

"What a lovely cover." She admired. "Is this free?"

"Yes. The books are provided for the club. You will need to have read it before we start on the 14th December." Nora explained.

"Oh I will do."

"Is that book for sale?" A man asked, shuffling close to Miss Raven.

She spun aside possessively.

"No!" She hissed.

"Why not?!" The man demanded.

"It's privately printed." Nora told him.

"Where can I get one?"

"It will be reprinted next year in a new edition. You can check back and see if it is available in about a year." Nora explained, plotting to republish the novels since there appeared to be an interest in them.

"I could be dead by then." He scowled. "Just these then."

"COME ALONG POPPET!" Miss Raven screeched towards the back of the shop, making everyone flinch.

"Oh, I didn't see Mrs Raven come in." Nora said, ignoring Felix who dived under the counter, sniggering.

Heather was staring, transfixed.

"She did. She went upstairs. Perhaps you could…"

At that moment there was a loud bang, followed by several more, like an enormous round ornament was rolling down the stairs. Nora held still. In fact, it was

Mrs Raven rolling down the stairs, like an enormous round ornament.

"Help…me…help…me…can you…can you…help me…" Mrs Raven's loud whispering called.

Felix dissolved into silent hysterical laughter while Nora, Heather, Miss Raven and a man in his forties all rushed to help.

Mrs Raven lay in a crumpled heap with her legs in the air at the bottom of the staircase. She was wearing bloomers.

"POPPET!" Miss Raven screeched.

Nora looked around hastily, cringing and hoping they wouldn't be sued.

"Did you trip, Mrs Raven?" She sympathised, checking there were no protruding bones through the lumps of dumpy flesh sticking out at all angles.

"I…did…yes, can you…ask her if…ask her if…"

"I think we should call an ambulance." Heather said.

"I agree." Nora nodded.

"I'll do it." Heather hurried back into the front room.

"Mrs Raven. Can you tell me if you hurt anywhere?" Nora asked, worried.

Mrs Raven held out a ladybird book.

"Ask her if…ask her if…" She whispered hard.

"Poppet! Have you broken anything? Like your neck, Poppet?" Miss Raven asked frantically.

"I used to be a paramedic." The man in his forties revealed. He was swiftly and silently giving Mrs Raven a look and a feel all over. "I don't think there's any serious damage."

Nora sighed in relief.

Mrs Raven was staring at the handsome man running his hands all over her.

"Ask her if…" She whispered faintly and then swooned.

"Oh dear." Nora winced.

"I think that was because of me." The man said, standing up.

"POPPET! Can you hear me?!" Miss Raven shrieked.

A small crowd had gathered. People were craning their necks and leaning over the stair banisters from the floors above to see the spectacle. Nora noticed Spencer's long white hair over the top banister.

"Ambulance is on its way." Heather announced.

"Can we move her?" Nora asked the man with octopus hands.

"Probably best wait for the paramedics." He advised.

Miss Raven slapped her mother around the face.

"POPPET!"

"I think your mother will be alright. She's probably in shock." Octopus-Hands said.

Miss Raven fluttered her eyelashes at him. Nora and Heather stared.

"Thank you kind sir." Miss Raven cooed. "How very reassuring you are."

"Er...no problem." Octopus-Hands smiled awkwardly.

Nora was sure she could hear Felix sniggering.

"Nothing to see here ladies and gents." Nora told the crowd.

Someone took a photo with their iPhone.

Nora hastily covered Mrs Raven's legs.

"Excuse me. How long will she be?" A man asked.

He stood at the top of the stairs at the head of a queue, holding armfuls of books. One dislodged and plonked down each step like a slinky until it landed on Mrs Raven's unconscious head.

Miss Raven was too busy simpering over Octopus-Hands to notice.

"Well, that depends on how long it takes for the ambulance to come. May I ask you to kindly be patient?" Nora called up.

There were murmurs and objections. A large man shoved through and began down.

"I can get past easily." He announced.

Nora and Heather watched, aghast, as he stepped over Mrs Raven. Other people copied him, including Spencer, and Nora grimaced, winced and cringed as several boots skimmed Mrs Raven's face.

"People are grotesque." Heather said when the last person had clambered selfishly by.

"I agree." Nora nodded, placing Heather's scarf under Mrs Raven's head.

Mrs Raven began to snore.

They waited for ten minutes for the ambulance, turning customers away who moaned about not being able to go upstairs, and helping people climb over Mrs Raven's legs as they went to and from the Bargain Book Yard.

Finally, a man and a woman in green jumpsuits arrived.

"Hello there. Ah, dear, let's take a look." The man said kindly.

"She rolled down the steps." Miss Raven said.

Nora blinked and stared. Octopus-Hands had an arm around Miss Raven's shoulders and looked very cosy.

"What's her name?"

"Mrs Raven." Nora volunteered.

"Mrs Raven? Mrs Raven, dear? Can you hear me?" The man asked.

"What's her first name?" The female paramedic asked.

"Delilah." Miss Raven said.

Nora and Heather stared.

"Delilah? Delilah?"

Nora couldn't help but think of the Tom Jones's song 'Delilah'. It started to play in her mind.

"Ask her if..." Mrs Raven suddenly whispered.

She was still grasping her ladybird book.

"Ah, Delilah dear." The male paramedic smiled.

They asked her questions, checked her over, performed some medical assessments and finally decided to help her onto a gurney and take her for a more thorough look over in the ambulance. This was a bit of an ordeal and Mrs Raven broke wind loudly several times until finally she was wheeled off with Miss Raven and Octopus-Hands following.

Nora and Heather returned to the front room. Felix was in tears.

"I'm sorry. Eeek. Guilty emoji." He apologised, wiping his eyes. "It was the trumpeting exit that got to me."

Nora was biting back her own smile.

"Well it's all sorted now. The paramedics don't think she broke anything but will just have some bruises. We should write it in the accident report book." She said.

Felix leapt up.

"I'll do it!" He volunteered.

Heather served some customers, watching Felix take a thin book from inside the meter cupboard above the heater and alarm pad. He sat back down and picked up a pen.

"Date." He read and filled it in.

"Time?" He checked his watch. "Approximately four fifteen by my estimation." He grinned and wrote it down.

"Details of incident." He read and cleared his throat, saying as he wrote. "There was a loud bang and then the sound of a being rolling down the flight of steps. I'd better check how many stairs." He got up and headed out the back.

Nora laughed.

"Thirteen steps. Unlucky for some." Felix said, coming back and writing it down. "The being was an elderly lady, of approximately one hundred years of age, called Mrs Raven."

"Delilah Raven." Nora added.

Felix sniggered.

"Delilah Raven." He amended. "She had taken a tumble and landed in a heap at the bottom on the flagstones. Which are currently cold because of the time of year."

"Are they?"

"I expect so." Felix smirked.

"It was decided to call the ambulance service. Heather Jolly dialled 999 and called for an ambulance team which arrived ten minutes later. After giving the subject the all over, they fetched a gurney with a squeaky wheel, loaded the subject on to it and wheeled her off. We hope she is not being taken for experimentation or euthanizing."

"Have you really written that?" Heather asked, passing a tall man, whose head skimmed the ceiling, his bag of books.

"Yes. Georgina never reads it." Felix nodded.

"We write lots of things in there." Nora explained with a smirk.

"The last entry was when Roger discovered there were no more toilet rolls. He used some pages from an old book and complained about a rash." Felix said.

Heather squealed with laughter.

They spent the next ten minutes reading through the old entries in The Secondhand Bookworm accident report book which included Cal getting a splinter, Betty dropping a book on someone's knee, a cup of tea being too hot, and an old man falling flat on his face in the history room. Felix then put it back in the cupboard.

"By the way, I never got a chance to tell you, but I offered two free books to people buying over ten from the Bargain Book Yard earlier."

"Oh! I had a big argument with a man about that."

"Did you let him have them?"

"Yes I did in the end because I thought it would be good to shift them all. I took another seven hundred pounds while Mrs Delilah Raven was taking a nap at the bottom of the stairs." Felix pointed out.

"Wow. Yes there was a constant stream of buyers treading all over her. I'll go and see how many books are left out there. We'll close up at five thirty."

"It's getting dark outside." Heather noticed.

"Go and drum up some business." Nora smirked.

Heather set off outside.

Nora was shocked at the state of the Bargain Book Yard. She spent a while turning several books to face outwards on the bare shelves but as she did so, they were snatched up and carried away. People continued to arrive and leave with armfuls of books. Nora was amazed and worn out after only fifteen minutes.

At five o'clock a regular customer arrived. He was known as the Map-Boy. The Map-Boy was a teenage boy with an obsession with the old Ordnance Survey maps. He made a bee-line for the section in the bottom stairwell and proceeded to take out, unfold and examine endless maps, muddling up the order and making a huge mess while saying 'Aaaaaah, ahhhhh" over and over again.

"Hello." Nora said politely as she passed him to go back into the front room.

He stared at her through his thick rimmed glasses and promptly sat on the floor, surrounded by open maps.

"The villainous Map-Boy is here?" Heather asked.

She was wearing her coat, gloves and bobble hat and holding a white paper bag.

"How did you know?" Nora sighed.

"I can hear him. Ugh. That section was so nicely sorted." She lamented.

"Something to do on Monday." Nora tried to be positive. "What's in the bag?"

"I was herding people into the shop like a collie dog herding sheep when I noticed these mince pies in the delicatessen window." Heather said.

Felix sat up.

"Oooh, the pies from the deli are so scrummy." He gasped.

"I didn't get you one."

"Crumbs." Felix looked devastated.

"Just kidding." Heather laughed.

Felix looked delighted once more.

Nora picked one out of the bag.

"Thanks, Heather."

"I actually bought ten. I thought the Duke might like to sample one tonight." Heather explained in a low voice.

"I'm sure he will." Nora agreed, taking a bite and closing her eyes as she chewed happily.

"Hello."

A dumpy man with slicked back grey hair, a large nose, tiny eyes and wearing a white t-shirt and black jeans, arrived.

Nora stopped chewing.

"Trade." He said, throwing one of his business cards onto the counter as he passed.

Nora, Heather and Felix stared.

He gave them a look before heading off upstairs.

"He's horrible." Nora then said in a quiet tone. "His name is Iris and he says he's trade and he has a card, but he haggles aggressively for more than ten percent off. Oh, he's a horrible little man."

"Oooeerr." Felix grimaced.

"Oh dear." Heather worried.

They heard him stomping about in the room above them.

"Isn't Iris a woman's name?" Felix asked.

"I think it's his surname." Nora explained.

"Or…maybe he was a woman." Felix suggested and sniggered.

Nora checked her watch.

"I want to go home now." She decided.

"Shall we start bringing things in?" Heather volunteered, popping the last of her mince pie into her mouth.

"Yes, we could do. I can hear loads of people in the Bargain Book Yard."

"I'll deal with them." Felix said, shovelling the last of his mince pie in.

At that moment the Map-Boy shot past, almost bowling Felix over, and disappeared into the darkness. Nora and Heather stared.

A Skype message arrived from Seatown.

'Can you do a Wordsworth stock check and send it through please? – Cara xx'

"Noooooooooo!" Nora bewailed.

"Oh crumbs. They take ages." Felix said.

With a sigh, Nora printed out the list of all the new Wordsworth paperbacks they ordered and decided to do the stock check herself. She left Heather wheeling in the postcard spinners followed by heaps of people and Felix serving a row of customers instead of going to the Bargain Book Yard.

On the next floor landing, Nora saw that the Wordsworth paperbacks had had a huge rummage and there were many gaps. Nora could hear Iris shuffling in the gardening section in the front room so threw a scowl in his direction. Once before the Wordsworth paperbacks, Nora began to count how many copies they had of each title and write the result next to the titles on her list, having to redo several as she discovered that they had been rummaged out of order.

"You have a run of books about fruit trees. Fifteen volumes in total; illustrated and priced at eight pounds fifty each." Iris said, appearing on the landing like a large gargoyle. "In total they come to one hundred and twenty seven pounds and fifty pence. The ten percent off you offer for trade makes it one hundred and fourteen pounds and seventy five pence. I'll buy them from you for eighty pounds."

Nora stared.

"I know the ones you mean. I'm sorry, but there were actually about twenty five of those and they have been selling well at the full price. I would be happy to do them for you at the ten percent trade discount but…"

"That's not enough." Iris snapped.

He flicked back his hair and advanced on Nora menacingly. Nora stepped back towards the Wordsworth cases.

"I would pay eighty pounds and no more."

"That's a shame." Nora replied, refusing to let him bully her. She turned and went back to her list.

With a start, Nora felt Iris's hand on her shoulder. She was forcibly spun around to face his beetroot red countenance.

"Ten percent is not enough for trade!" He hissed.

"Remove your hand from me, please." Nora requested politely, but she felt her knees starting to shake.

Iris did so but his small eyes flashed and he leaned closer to Nora.

"Eighty pounds is my final offer!" He breathed forebodingly.

His face was very close to hers. Nora swallowed hard.

"Excuse me." A young man stepped out of the children's room behind Nora.

He had been listening to Nora and Iris and had obviously decided to step in.

Nora looked at him.

"Can you show me where the Enid Blyton books are, please?" He asked, giving Iris a look. "I'm looking for some for my daughter."

Iris scowled.

"Oh…erm, yes, of course." Nora nodded, moving away from Iris.

He glared after her before heading back to the gardening section in the front room.

"I thought I'd rescue you from that maniac." The young man said.

"Oh thank you." Nora appreciated, fanning her hot face. "He's always like that."

"You should kick him out and ban him." The man suggested.

"I think I might do that." Nora nodded, still shaking slightly.

"Are you alright?"

"Yes, he's just very confrontational."

"I'll have a word with him if you like?"

They heard Iris stomping down the stairs.

"Thanks, but I think he's leaving." Nora appreciated. The man smiled.

"Here are the Enid Blyton books." Nora indicated.

"Oh, I found them already. I was just trying to rescue you." The man admitted with a warm smile.

Nora smiled too.

"Thanks. I appreciate it."

He grinned and Nora went back to checking the Wordsworth paperbacks, scowling over Iris. As she reached the end of her list she became aware of raised voices downstairs. Frowning, Nora headed back down the stairs, stepping over a mountain of Ordnance Survey maps on the floor at the bottom. When Nora reached the front room she saw Iris, red faced and prodding Felix in the chest across the counter.

"Excuse me!" Nora interrupted firmly, outraged.

Felix looked mortified and hurried to hide behind Nora.

"This man won't give me more than ten percent off these books!" Iris almost shouted.

Nora saw that he had carried all fifteen volumes of the fruit books down.

"That is because as a policy we only offer ten percent off our books to trade customers and I believe even that is generous." Nora defended.

Heather was serving a customer who was staring in alarm.

"I demand that you telephone the owner!" Iris shook his fist.

"No." Nora refused.

He stood puffing and staring at her threateningly.

"Mr Iris. You can purchase these books for one hundred and ten pounds. That would be a little more of a discount than ten percent for you. But that is my final offer." Nora said firmly, feeling her knees shaking again in the face of such bullying.

He pursed his lips angrily and stood thinking about it.

"One five!" He attempted to barter.

"One ten." Nora held her ground.

After a long moment, Iris relented.

"One ten it effing is then!" He said coarsely and Nora gasped.

There was long silence.

"Would you like bags?" Felix asked from behind Nora.

"Yes!" Iris spat.

Felix helped Nora bag up the books as Nora did the transaction once Heather had finished her sale. Iris snatched his card from Nora and demanded a written receipt. Patiently, Nora wrote out the details and handed it to him. He gathered up the bags of books and stomped off without another word.

When he had gone, Nora, Felix and Heather sighed in relief.

"What a horror!" Felix exclaimed.

"He was a monster." Heather agreed. "You should get Georgina to ban him!"

"Hmm, it is tempting." Nora nodded. "I need a stiff drink."

"Shall I tell the Duke? He could ban him from the town." Heather suggested.

That made Nora grin.

"I think he would for you." Felix nodded. "Oh, get him to!"

Nora laughed.

At five thirty, Heather closed the door, removed all the Black Friday signs and put Nora's Book Club poster on the window of the door in pride of place. The last of the customers were shoed out and Nora, Heather and Felix stood looking at the Bargain Book Yard.

"Amazing." Felix breathed.

"Incredible." Heather nodded.

"I hope Georgina immigrates before the next Black Friday. I don't want to go through that again." Nora said, half serious.

The shelves had been cleared so that the equivalent of only about three boxes of stock remained in total. The table that had collapsed under the weight of the reading man leaned against the bolted door, so the group cleared the last of the display books from the other tables and placed the books on the shelves, tidied up, turned off the pumpkin face lights which had almost expired, had a sweep and stood back to admire their work.

"Hopefully the rest will sell tomorrow." Nora said.

"Will Georgina open the yard up tomorrow then?" Heather asked.

"Oh, I expect so. She might as well for one last day and it's shocking how many customers they get on a Sunday sometimes."

"Let's hope she clears the lot." Felix agreed.

They locked the door on the Bargain Book Yard. Heather washed up and Felix checked upstairs and turned the lights off while Nora sent through the Wordsworth list via Skype so the ones they were low on could be reordered on Monday morning, first thing, by the Seatown branch.

"What an amazing end to the week." Felix said as he added up the final figure.

The shop telephone began to ring so Heather answered it.

"Oh hello, Georgina. Yes, we're still here. An amazing day, yes." Heather was smiling. "Oh thank you! That's very kind. Yes, I'll pass her over."

Heather handed Nora the phone.

"Another good day I hear. Cara told me the final figures." Georgina's smiling voice congratulated.

"Yes. Well done on the Black Friday idea. It's been mammoth."

"And thank you for all your hard work. I'm writing you a cheque for five hundred pounds."

Nora almost fell over.

"Really?! That is so generous of you!"

"Both you and Cara deserve good bonuses this week after all your efforts." Georgina said. "Fluffy! Get off of Chubby's head! Please give Felix and Heather a thirty pound bonus each for today too."

"I will. Thank you, Georgina."

"Have you put your Book Club poster back up, yet?"

"Yes, it looks very inviting."

"I'll try and get you some decent members tomorrow. I'm working with Paperback Pam for the day again so I shall try and get her to do other things rather than just the paperback room."

"We tidied up the Bargain Book Yard in case you want to open it tomorrow. There are about three boxfuls of stock left, all displayed on the shelves. I did an eighty percent discount for the last hour today."

"Well done! I'll keep it eighty percent for tomorrow then and hopefully that will get rid of all the tat! Have a nice evening."

Nora thought of the Duke of Cole and smiled.

"I will. Bye."

Georgina bade goodbye and they rang off. Nora then gave Felix and Heather thirty pounds each from the till.

"Where's yours?" Heather asked.

"Mine is coming in cheque form." Nora said.

"Ooooh. Well done." Felix smiled, shrugging into his coat.

They finished cashing up, packed away, turned off the computer and the lights, set the alarm and fled the shop.

A woman was waiting outside.

"Hello. I've been reading your poster for your Book Club." She said as Nora locked up The Secondhand Bookworm.

"Oh. Yes. Are you interested?" Nora smiled.

"No. Looks good though." The woman replied and wandered off humming.

Felix sniggered behind his hands.

Nora and Heather stared.

"Probably a good thing." Heather said with a small smirk.

"Quite." Nora agreed, watching the woman skip across the road.

"Thanks for today, Felix." Nora appreciated.

"Looking forward to reading this!" He said, holding up his copy of 'The Missing Candlesticks'.

"Make sure you finish it by the fourteenth. And have some exciting reflections ready for us all to hear."

"I will." He assured, gave a wave and headed off to where he had parked his car by the moat.

Nora and Heather began up the hill.

"It's very exciting."

"The Book Club?"

"Yes." Heather nodded. "I wonder how many people there will be."

"I'm not sure. But I'm going to keep it to no more than ten."

"Do you think the Duke will remain incognito?"

"Possibly." Nora smiled.

"Before he comes tonight, shall we have a game of Wizzingball on the Jupiter Cube?" Heather suggested.

"You twisted my arm." Nora grinned and, linking arms with her sister, she set off up the hill to spend the evening with the Duke of Cole, wondering what events her Book Club at The Secondhand Bookworm would have in store!

THE END

EMILY JANE BEVANS

ALSO IN THE SERIES

'The Secondhand Bookworm'
'Nora and The Secondhand Bookworm'
'Christmas at The Secondhand Bookworm'
'Summer at The Secondhand Bookworm'
'Halloween at The Secondhand Bookworm'

Available in paperback and Kindle 2018

Coming soon

'Book Club at The Secondhand Bookworm;

Watch for more novels in the Bookworm series

Also by the author

'House of Villains'
Available now from Amazon

ABOUT THE AUTHOR

Emily Jane Bevans lives on the south coast of England. For ten years she worked in, and helped to manage, a family chain of antiquarian bookshops in Sussex. She is the co-founder and co-director of a UK based Catholic film production apostolate 'Mary's Dowry Productions'. She writes, edits, produces, directs, narrates and sometimes acts for the company's numerous historical and religious films on the lives of the Saints and English Martyrs. She also likes to write contemporary and historical fiction.

MARY'S DOWRY PRODUCTIONS

Mary's Dowry Productions is a Catholic Film
Production Apostolate founded in 2007 to bring the lives
of the Saints and English Martyrs, English Catholic
heritage and history to film and DVD. Mary's Dowry
Productions' unique film production style has been
internationally praised for not only presenting facts,
biographical information and historical details but a
prayerful and spiritual film experience. Many of the
films of Mary's Dowry Productions have been broadcast
on EWTN, BBC and SKY.
For a full listing of films and more information visit:

www.marysdowryproductions.org

EMILY JANE BEVANS

Made in the USA
Columbia, SC
31 January 2021

32091622R00143